THE SEXY ONE

by Lauren Blakely

ALSO BY LAUREN BLAKELY

The Caught Up in Love Series (Each book in this series follows a different couple so each book can be read separately, or enjoyed as a series since characters crossover)

Caught Up in Her (A short prequel novella to *Caught Up in Us*)
Caught Up In Us
Pretending He's Mine
Trophy Husband
Stars in Their Eyes

Standalone Novels
BIG ROCK
Mister O
Well Hung
The Sexy One
Full Package (Jan 2017)
The Hot One (March 2017)
Joy Stick (Spring 2017)
Far Too Tempting
21 Stolen Kisses
Playing With Her Heart (A standalone SEDUCTIVE NIGHTS spin-off novel about Jill and Davis)

The No Regrets Series
The Thrill of It
The Start of Us
Every Second With You

The Seductive Nights Series
First Night (Julia and Clay, prequel novella)
Night After Night (Julia and Clay, book one)
After This Night (Julia and Clay, book two)
One More Night (Julia and Clay, book three)
A Wildly Seductive Night (Julia and Clay novella)
Nights With Him (A standalone novel about Michelle and Jack)
Forbidden Nights (A standalone novel about Nate and Casey)

The Sinful Nights Series
Sweet Sinful Nights
Sinful Desire
Sinful Longing
Sinful Love

The Fighting Fire Series
Burn For Me (Smith and Jamie)
Melt for Him (Megan and Becker)
Consumed By You (Travis and Cara)

The Jewel Series
The Sapphire Affair
The Sapphire Heist

ABOUT

Let me count the ways why falling into forbidden love is not my wisest move . . .

1. She works with me every single day.

Did I mention she's gorgeous, sweet, kind and smart?

2. She works in my home.

Playing with my five-year-old daughter. Teaching my little girl. Cooking for my princess. Which means . . .

3. She's the nanny.

And that makes her completely off-limits . . . But it doesn't stop me from wanting her. All of her.

* * *

The other nannies in this city don't call him the Sexy One for nothing. My boss, the amazingly wonderful single father to the girl I take care of every day is ridiculously hot, like movie star levels with those arms, and those eyes, and that body. Not to mention, the way he dotes on his little girl melts me all over. But what really makes my knees weak are the times when his gaze lingers on me. In secret. When no one else is around.

I can't risk my job for a chance at something more . . . can I? But I don't know how to resist him much longer either . . .

CHAPTER ONE

Abby

Attraction is a funny thing. It's chemical, right? At first it's all snap, crackle, pop—a cocktail of desire. And what an intoxicating mix it is. It's a rush, it's a thrill . . . it's pure exhilaration uncorked. It makes you giddy. It makes you feel like you can run a marathon and still scale a building even after the twenty-sixth mile is complete.

And I really hate running.

Attraction can turn ordinarily sensible men and women into single-minded hunters, silly fools, and sometimes into lucky lovers.

When the feeling is mutual, most of the time everyone is happy and they go about their merry business. No one hears about these couplings, because little gets in the way. Good for them, and tra-la-la-dee-dah.

But sometimes, attraction is unrequited, and sometimes we don't even admit it exists. I'm about to vehemently deny it, as the other nannies and babysitters scoot closer on the bleachers and whisper.

Simon walks onto the deck at the pool where his daughter takes swim lessons. The reaction is predictable as clockwork. The redheaded sitter of the unruly twin girls fluffs her hair; the brunette with the cat eye glasses crosses her tanned, toned legs that go on forever; and the petite Australian nanny with her ponytail of silky black hair just gasps.

All eyes follow the man as he strides past the deep end, looking too gorgeous to be real.

"How do you manage working for him?" Ponytail Aussie whispers to me in a hushed breath.

"He's easy to work for," I say, though I know that's not what she's asking.

The real question comes next, landing in the chlorinated air.

"Seriously," the leggy one says. I'm jealous of her. I'll admit it. I'm a short girl, and I would love to borrow her legs for a night. I'd swap them out for my boobs, and that's a more than fair trade, because what I lack in height, I make up for in the girls. "How do you work with all that hotness?" she continues, prodding. "If you looked up 'hot single dad' in the dictionary, you'd find his picture."

Yeah.

He is.

He's the prize in the available dad sweepstakes.

Because . . .

Six foot three. Broad shoulders. Flat stomach. Trim waist. Square jawline. Hint of stubble. Dark blond hair.

Light blue eyes. And a smile that makes you melt into a puddle of lust.

Oh, and get this. He's also a sharp-dressed man, and that's my weakness. Charcoal slacks, shiny shoes, and those tailored shirts that fit deliciously. You know, the kind where the fabric just slides into the waistband of his pants, and you can't help but think *how is it your belly does a perfect imitation of a washboard, and can I please conduct some firmness tests on it? For the sake of science, of course.*

When handsomeness was handed out, Simon Travers landed more than a few extra helpings. The man snagged someone else's share, too. And another's and another's.

But that's not all he's got going on, and I'm dying to tell the other women that there's more to him than meets the eye. So much more.

He's sweet, kind, smart, funny, and good. So damn good. And, for a bonus prize, add in that he's an amazing father. That's some sexy kryptonite right there.

Only, if I tried to explain all those other traits, they'd *know*. They'd sniff me out in the snap of the fingers. They'd see the attraction written on my face, hear it in my words.

I can't let on how I feel about Simon, because I've spent the last seven months taking care of his adorable five-year-old daughter. And I've spent the last six months, three weeks, and four days keeping the cat of all that attraction tucked in a neat, sealed, airtight bag.

(*That's a metaphor, obviously. No cats were harmed in the telling of this tale.*)

And for the math wizards of the world, that means it took me three days on the clock to like the guy.

Fine, I'll admit that's hardly any time at all, but he's just that likeable.

That also means I spend all my working days fighting this need to fling myself at him. It's not as though he's ever given me a sign that he's interested, so call this crush unrequited. I've learned to live with it. I've come to accept it, the same way you accept having a spray of freckles across your nose, or curly hair that'll never straighten. It's a fact of my existence now, and like the freckles and the curls, I deal with it when I arrive at work, when I leave work, and when I meet him at various places in the city, including here.

In her dolphin-decorated one-piece, Simon's daughter, Hayden, splashes around the shallow end of the pool with the other kids and the swim instructor. When she surfaces, she pushes her goggles up her face and spots her hero. The kid beams, her smile as wide as the sky as she shouts, "Daddy! Come see me dive!"

"On my way!" Turning the corner at the deep end, he walks past, waving as we watch the kids, and, let's be honest, ogle him.

His eyes meet mine next. "Hey, Abby," he says, with an easy grin.

My pulse speeds up, and I wave back. But I don't blush. I don't stammer. See? I live with this attraction, and I've mastered the art of self-control, revealing nothing as we hand-off the kid here at the pool today. "Hey there."

He nods at his adoring fans. "Hello, ladies."

That's all it takes. Two words from the hottest guy around, and the hearts, they're all aflutter as they wave back. He walks on by, crouching at the edge of the pool to say hi to his little girl and drop a quick kiss on her forehead.

Yup, his love for his girl makes him even hotter.

Leggy Lady leans in, pats my shoulder, and deadpans, "Nope. I'm not jealous of you whatsoever. Not one bit. Not at all."

I shake my head, trying to dismiss the idea. "The only thing to be jealous about is that I'm two months away from paying off my college loans," I say with a wry smile.

She narrows her eyes. "Now I really hate you."

As I steal a glance at Simon, *hate* is the furthest word from my mind. The four-letter word that's now front and center is *work*.

Tomorrow night, he'll be working late. Which means I can snag a few minutes when he comes home just with him. I've learned to treasure those moments here and there when I get to talk to him, to know him, to learn more about him. The times when it's only us.

That's the funniest thing of all about attraction. It can be so torturous, but you can look forward to it so much. It's an exquisite kind of torment.

It can drive you in everything, including how much I'm looking forward to tomorrow night.

CHAPTER TWO

Simon

"Looks like squirrel is on the dinner menu," Abby calls to me as I leave the bedroom, looping a wine-red tie around my neck.

"I mentioned he was an inventive chef, but I'm not sure he's *that* inventive," I tease as I round the corner into the kitchen. "Besides, I'm pretty sure I told you it's a Brazilian restaurant I'm trying to back. Not a rodent one."

She shakes her head, her honey-colored hair curling over her shoulders. It's long and shimmery; sometimes she wears it in a French braid, sometimes in a twisty thing, sometimes in a ponytail, and sometimes down. Not that I'm paying close attention to her hair. I couldn't tell you she wore it pinned up earlier today when she'd first arrived at my home, and all I could think about was her neck and how her skin might taste if I brushed my lips along the column of her throat. Or that she had it pulled back in a loose ponytail yesterday, making her look younger and even prettier. Or how the day before that she ran a hand through her wild, wavy hair and I couldn't help but wonder how those soft strands felt to touch.

No, I don't notice every little detail about Abby Becker. Not at all.

"I'm talking about the eagles. You already forgot about the eagles?" She points to the screen of her iPad as I join her at the kitchen counter, adjusting the silk knot of my tie.

"I could never forget the eagles," I say, and it's true. I've checked them out a couple of times during the last few days, though Abby's done most of the eagle viewing. She's a tiny bit obsessed with nature documentaries. I don't mean obsessed in a bad way. They're her thing, and so they've become Hayden's thing, since Abby spends so much time with her, taking care of her when I work. Last week, Abby discovered a webcam the American Bald Eagle Association had focused on a pair of bald eagle mates in a nest high up in a poplar tree in the National Arboretum in Washington D.C. Two baby eagles hatched a few days ago, and Abby and Hayden have been logging in regularly, watching the mom as she sits on the tiny birds, as she grooms them, and as she feeds them.

"Mr. Eagle usually brings fish deliveries, but tonight he brought Mrs. Eagle a squirrel," Abby says, her amber-flecked eyes sparkling with excitement.

"Must be a special night. Because you know the saying?"

"Which one is that?"

"Nothing says true love like a squirrel."

"It's the complete and absolute proof of his devotion," she says with a laugh. "I took a screenshot to show Hayden in the morning."

On the tablet, a huge bald eagle is feeding her two babies, tugging at the meat between her claws with her beak and dropping it in hungry mouths. It's ridiculously adorable and completely badass at the same time. Hayden will love it. She conked out early tonight. Another swimming lesson late in the day did the trick, sending her to the land of nod ahead of schedule.

"This is Mother Nature at its finest, capturing these animals doing their thing." Abby parks her chin in her hand and watches the evening feast in the poplar tree, wonder in her eyes. I lean closer. My shoulder is next to hers, a mere sliver of space between us. No, this is not the fulfillment of all my dreams about Abby, but I can't deny that being this near to her is borderline arousing. Could be because it's been a while. Could be because she smells like vanilla and sunshine. But it could also be because I've been wildly in lust with her for precisely seven months longer than I should.

It was kind of a first-day thing for me. Wish I could say otherwise, but that's the truth. Insta-lust. Trouble is, it's morphed into a helluva lot more than lust in all this time she's spent in my home, with my family, with my kid.

Admiration. Fondness. The real deal.

It's turned into exactly what I cannot have.

A big thing for the nanny.

If I could roll my eyes at myself, I would. Maybe even kick myself. But I can't, so I zone in on the screen instead.

The mama eagle drops a piece of food into one eaglet's beak, then the other.

"I guess we call that mouth-to-mouth squirrel delivery, and it is pretty awesome," I say, because you'd have to be heartless not to find this webcam footage fascinating. The big bird gathers the babies underneath her when the feast is over, keeping them warm. I point to the uneaten portion of the dinner. "They have enough left over for a few more meals. She should really put that in Tupperware."

"I'm sure Mr. Eagle is at the market, picking some up right now. It's important to keep it fresh," she says in mock seriousness. Then she turns to me. "Want me to let you know when they go back for seconds?"

"Absolutely. Please send me a full report on the next eaglet feeding." I look at my wristwatch. "I need to head to my dinner. I should be back by eleven."

"If you need to stay later to entertain Gabriel, it's totally fine. I have a book, and my Italian app to work through," she says, tapping her iPad. She already speaks four languages and is learning a fifth. When I interviewed her for the job, she told me she spent her junior year of college in Barcelona on a study abroad program. She grew up knowing Spanish, but wanted to master it, and she has. She offered to teach some basics to Hayden, and now my daughter is picking up a few new phrases. That's one of the many perks of working with someone like Abby.

"I'll definitely be back on time," I say, because I don't want this dinner with the hot new chef everyone is wooing to last forever, and because I need to be considerate of Abby's time. She works full-time for me, since I have primary custody of my daughter.

Abby scowls as she circles her finger in the direction of my chest. "You're not going to wear *that*, are you?"

Her tone makes it clear the correct answer is no, but I have no clue if she means the pressed white shirt, or the silk tie.

"And which sartorial item evokes your displeasure?"

"The tie," she says crisply. "It's all wrong."

"Why, may I ask?"

"It's too Wall Street."

"I did work on Wall Street for a decade."

She nods several times. "It shows. That tie makes it abundantly clear you've spent plenty of hours with Standard & Poor's," she says with a smirk. "Not like you're an I-left-Wall-Street-to-back-hip-eateries investor."

And folks, this is reason number 547 why I can't shake this desire. Because she's so goddamn direct, and it's a fucking turn-on. After my ex's falseness, Abby's honesty is refreshing and downright alluring.

"Which tie should I wear then?" I ask, and for a moment, I nearly let myself believe I'm asking like a man seeking input from the woman he's with. As if she's going to step closer, undo the tie, and toss it on the couch. As if she's going to run her hands down the front of my shirt and say *Skip the dinner—have me instead.*

I'd miss the dinner in the blink of an eye. I'd have her all night long, again and again, and send her soaring in pleasure.

But I can't let my brain hop too far from my reality.

We're not a couple. We're not together. She's my daughter's twenty-six-year-old nanny. I'm her thirty-four-year-old employer. Abby is bright and beautiful and funny and smart and so fucking sexy, and she's *only* giving me advice on clothing because she's one of the most upfront and caring people I've ever met, not because she's playing house.

"No tie," she answers, her eyes fixed on my attire.

"None at all?" I ask, because I like the fact that she's looking at me, that she's thinking about me.

She purses her lips, drawing my attention to them, all shiny and glossy. She shakes her head. "You don't need to be a tie guy anymore. Besides, I like the tieless look."

"Why's that?"

She straightens her shoulders and gestures to me. "It says confidence. It says you're so cool you don't even need neckwear."

I narrow my eyes, adopting a debonair simmer. "Guy. Tieless Guy," I say in my best over-the-top-suave James Bond tone.

She laughs. "Perfect. Though I'd have pegged you more in the Chris Hemsworth type of role." She quirks up the corners of her lips. "You're a dead ringer."

Oh, yeah.

That is a compliment.

And I'll gladly eat it up.

"On that note, I should go."

"Good luck tonight," she says, upbeat and cheery. Her eyes meet mine, and for a few seconds they linger. Neither one of us says anything. I just enjoy the view of her gorgeous face.

That gorgeous, *untouchable* face.

I repeat that word silently. *Untouchable.* She's off-limits to me.

Her tone shifts to something softer as she adds, "And if the eagles get hungry again, I'll send you a message, Simon."

My breath hitches, just from hearing her say my name like that. I swallow, my throat dry. How can I be so wound up at the thought she *might* send me a text about a bird of prey eating? I know the answer, of course. It's as old as time.

I want her.

I pop into Hayden's room. She's sound asleep under the covers, her wild brown hair fanned out over the lavender pillowcase. I press a soft kiss to her forehead and run my fingers lightly over her hair. "Good night, little dolphin."

I step away, quietly close the door, and return to the living room, grabbing my phone.

"See you in a few hours," I say to Abby, who's settled into the couch with her iPad.

"See you later, Guy, Tieless Guy," she says, and waves goodbye from her spot amongst the soft pillows. She looks good curled up on the couch, like she belongs here. Like she's mine and she'll be staying the night.

I'd like to smack myself right now, because it's so cliché —the single dad who's got it bad for the nanny.

I shake my head in the building's mirrored elevator and mutter, "Get it together, man."

I might want her, but I sure as hell can't have her. Something I remind myself of later that night, when a text from her lands on my phone.

CHAPTER THREE

Simon

Gabriel points to the angel food cake. "This tastes like a sweet pillow melting in your mouth, does it not?"

"Like a blueberry pillow," I add since the cake is covered in blueberries and blueberry sauce.

He brings his fingers to his lips and kisses the tips. "It is home, plus flare. That's what I want. I want this feeling in Gabriel's on Christopher," he says, since he's already picked a spot in the Village for the new restaurant he wants to open—his first in Manhattan, coming on the heels of his wildly successful eateries in Miami and Los Angeles. He's French and Brazilian, and his creations are a fusion of both cuisines.

He turns to the men in his entourage, and says something in French, his native language. It's rapid-fire, and makes me wish I fully understood what he's saying, rather than just a word here or there, especially when his goateed business manager says something to me about wine. Eduardo is soft-spoken, so the question is mostly lost. Gabriel steps in, and repeats what he said.

"Sure. More wine," I say, sliding over the glass, because more wine is always the right answer in the food business. The restaurant we're at tonight is a few blocks away from the one he wants to open.

Gabriel pours more of the cabernet, sets down the bottle, then flips his long, wild hair off his shoulders. This man is a rock-star chef in every sense of the word. The hair, the tattoos, and of course, the talent. As for me, I can boil water extremely well and order takeout or delivery even better, but I'm excellent at sniffing out talent. And Gabriel is the real deal.

The trouble is, after his victory on a popular reality TV cooking show, nearly every big restaurant investor in town has sniffed him out, too, and wants the chance to back his first Manhattan establishment, especially since it'll be the flagship for a much bigger business expansion into cookware, cookbooks, and more. That's why I've spent the last few weeks buried in paperwork, developing the proposal that I hope will win his business.

We chat for a few more minutes about New York and food. "Manhattan needs your panache, Gabriel," I tell him, as my phone buzzes faintly in my pocket. I can't look now, since I want to give them my full attention. Besides, if there were an emergency with Hayden, Abby would call rather than text. "We've been sorely lacking in the sort of style you're known for, not to mention your daring in the kitchen."

"That makes me sad for your city," he says, his lips pulling into a playful frown.

"Exactly. But just imagine how happy you can make the taste buds in Manhattan."

He tosses his head back and laughs. "I can hear them crying out for me now. *Gabriel,*" he says, mimicking a host of adoring fans calling out his name. The thing is, he does have fans, and not only because he's masterful with a skillet and a knife. Women flock to him at his restaurants and his events, and I don't think they're after his lasagna recipe.

By the time the meal ends, I've got a good feeling that I can land this deal. We've skirted the subject of terms, but tonight's not the time for that. Besides, he knows my track record when it comes to investing, and what I bring to the table in capital as well as experience.

I take a final bite of the cake, then set down my fork, leaving the dessert half-finished.

"That is a sin," he says, narrowing his eyes at me.

I laugh. "True. My daughter would tell me there's always room in the dessert drawer."

Gabriel eyes the remaining slice of cake on the table. "Now, as your punishment for not finishing your dessert, you must take the extra piece home for your little girl."

I adopt a serious look. "Punishment accepted. And thank you. She'll be thrilled."

"Sweets are the way to a woman's heart," he adds.

Eduardo says something in French, and Gabriel laughs, translating as he taps his chest. "He tells me, isn't that my mantra?"

"And is it, Gabriel?" I toss back.

"I've been known to make a woman swoon with my crème brûlée," he says, shrugging sheepishly.

An idea strikes me—to take the extra piece to Abby.

I haven't taken dessert home for a woman in ages. My ex was one of those anti-sugar people, so treats were ver-boten. I never took any home for Miriam. She'd have scoffed at the offending item, and told me precisely how many calories were in a piece of pie, a slice of cake, a tart. She knew how to suck the fun out of dessert, of food, and come to think of it, of life in general.

On the crowded sidewalk outside the restaurant, we say good night. I shake hands with Gabriel, Eduardo, and the others, then hail a cab and let them take the first one. I grab the next taxi right behind it, and on the ride home I finally check my phone.

Abby: He brought her a fish!

I blink, and it takes me a second to process what Abby is talking about. Then it hits me. Mr. Eagle. She's up-dating me on the eagle. Okay, I'm not going to read any-thing into this, even though this is the first time we've texted about anything not related to work or schedules or kids.

But I grin as the car swings up Madison Avenue, and a warmth spreads through my body. I don't think it's from the wine. It's from what feels like the cusp of flirting.

Simon: Was it a big fish?

Look, I know we're talking about the predator's catch. Not other things that could be big. But still. It *is* big.

Her response arrives quickly.

Abby: Of course :) Mr. Eagle only takes home big prizes for his woman.

Absently, I tap the angel food cake in the takeout box next to me, then I write back.

Simon: As the man of the nest should. He is the hunter.

While the car streaks along the stretch of pavement, lights from late-night New York winking on and off, her name appears on my screen.

Abby: He's all about delivering on the You Had One Job premise.

That makes me laugh, and we keep up the playful banter a bit longer. Ten minutes later, I arrive at my building and head inside and up the elevator, buoyed by a slight buzz from the wine, but mostly from the texting. When the elevator stops on the eleventh floor, I'm keenly aware that this is one of life's pivotal moments.

No, I'm not the eagle, and this is not *National Geographic*.

But this is one of those moments when *something* happens—when this thing for Abby shifts from a simmer to a bubbling-over-the-pot boil. Start with nearly seven months of lust, add in a pair of eagles, chase it with a left-over dessert from a dinner with a chef, top it off with the absence of a wine-red tie.

I unlock the door and find her on the couch. Damn, she looks good in my home, with the lights dim and the quiet of the night wrapping its arms around her. She sets down her iPad, and I hold up the dessert.

"I brought a cake," I say proudly, as if I'd wrestled it from a fierce lion. "For you."

Okay, fine.

I'm totally the motherfucking hunter, and this is my prize for the woman I so badly want to woo.

CHAPTER FOUR

Abby

I'm not going to read anything into this. Even though—
hello, he brought me dessert. That's kind of a thing guys do
when they like a woman, right?

As I dig my fork into this unexpected treat, I flash back
on that lingering gaze before he left for the dinner, and
now to the way he said *for you.* A delicious possibility un-
furls in me. Perhaps this street isn't as one-way as I
thought. Maybe, just maybe, he's keen on me, too. I slide
the container a few inches across the counter, giddy from
these new thoughts jumping joyfully in my head, like
puppies bounding through a field of grass. "Do you want
to have some?"

"I think I may have already passed the legal limit for
cake consumption tonight," he says.

I wave the fork and correct him. "There's no limit for
cake. Harper and I have conducted many tests and have
proven as much."

"Not once were you able to reach the threshold?"

I shake my head. "Never. Each bite you take raises your
legal limit by one more bite."

He strokes his chin as if in deep thought. "So it's a rolling target? This cake limit?"

"It is. And we've studied it thoroughly, being cake fiends and all. It's entirely possible we were separated at birth when we were left in baskets outside Peace of Cake."

He knows my friend Harper. She's a magician, and he hired her to perform at Hayden's fifth birthday party last fall. At the time, Harper told me she had the tiniest crush on him, but that was way before she started spending more time with Nick. Now, the two of them are madly and inseparably in love. It's awesome.

What's also awesome is that Simon reached out to Harper for nanny advice. He took her out for coffee specifically to ask her for a recommendation, because she's good with kids. That's what he wanted for Hayden, and that's why he hired me.

"Was it your love of sweets that reunited you with your long lost magician sibling?" he asks, leaning against the island counter in the kitchen.

"That, and going to the same school." I take another bite. These are the late-night moments I savor. I love spending time with his daughter, but I also crave the stolen seconds when she's asleep, and we're adults, just talking to each other.

"College, right? I'm assuming you didn't go to high school with her since you're from Arizona, and she's from here."

I nod, impressed that he remembers all the details I've shared, then I add the year we graduated. He smirks and shakes his head as he laughs.

"What's so funny about that?"

"That was *only* four years ago." He taps his chest. "Whereas I finished twelve years ago."

I set down the fork, park my hands on the counter, and shoot him a steely stare. This is one of the reasons I like working with Simon. I can be playful with him. I can tease. He's not Mr. Serious, like my last employer. "I know how to do math."

Wait. Why is he bringing up the age difference? It's a curious detail to float out there. Maybe because it's late, or maybe because he brought me cake, or maybe because it's been a long time since I flirted, I decide to keep wandering along this path. This line of questioning is like a door sliding open, inviting me into a new kind of interaction with him, the one I secretly desire.

I inch closer. "And do you think you acquired all the knowledge in the world in those eight years you have on me?"

He scoffs. "God no. Sometimes I think I know less now than I did then."

My brow creases. "What do you mean?"

He rubs his hand across the back of his neck. His cuffs are rolled up, revealing his strong, toned forearms. He was a football player in high school, and a basketball star, too.

He's the rare high school jock who still looks fit and trim in his thirties. His arms are to-die-for. My hands itch to stroke those forearms, to explore his biceps, to hold on tight to his shoulders. In fact, for dessert, I'll skip the rest of the cake and take one order of sexy single dad, please.

"Just that there are things I might have done differently," he says in a softer tone, one laced with regret. His gaze drifts in the direction of Hayden's room. "But then again," he says, returning his focus to me, "I also think I wouldn't change a damn thing."

"I get it," I say quietly. "I totally do."

He flashes me a sweet smile. He doesn't talk about his ex-wife much, but the demise of their marriage wasn't too hard to figure out. Hayden's mother is involved with someone she works with, and from passing comments Simon has made, that relationship overlapped with their marriage.

He's never called Miriam a cheating bitch, but as far as I'm concerned, that's what she is. I've met her a few times, and she's quite accomplished at shooting dismissive glares at me and forgetting my name. She calls me Gabby every time she sees me. She's a great mom, though, and she's lovely with Hayden on the weekends she has her, so that's all anyone can ask for.

But I don't want to linger on her, even at the outskirts of this conversation. "How was your dinner?"

As I eat more of the cake, he tells me about his night. I like listening to him talk here in the dimly lit home, the clock skating toward midnight, the faint sounds of Manhattan floating through the windows.

"Gabriel is very outgoing, and easy to talk to. We didn't discuss the terms of any potential investment, but we all got along well," Simon says as he finishes sharing the details of his dinner.

"You're going to get the deal," I say with confidence.

He arches an eyebrow. "Can you see the future?"

"I didn't tell you that on my application? In addition to my amazing language skills and childcare talent, I read tea leaves. It's what everyone wants in their . . ." I trail off, for the first time feeling strange saying my job title. *Nanny.* It feels weird, maybe because this is the first night I've stayed this late and chatted with my boss as if we're a couple— me asking about his business dinner, him bringing me dessert, us texting on his route home—when we're so not.

My heart flutters, loving the possibilities painted in that picture.

"And the tea leaves point to Gabriel wanting my money?" Simon asks.

"Absolutely. How could he not? You know what you're doing. You're a wiz." I'm well aware that he has some kind of Midas touch when it comes to business. I've witnessed his talent in action on some of the phone calls that he takes at home, and I know his track record. The man wins deals.

I take another bite of the angel food cake. Silence spreads, and I think, but I can't be sure, that he watches me eat. That his eyes are on my lips as I bite into the soft cake. Maybe I'm imagining it, but the possibility heats me up. A warm, tingly feeling spreads to my shoulders then shoots down to my belly, and it happens again—one of those moments of connection where our eyes lock. It blots out all the reasons why we're a bad idea.

Because my body says we'd be oh-so-good.

My heart squeezes, and goosebumps rise on my skin. The air between us crackles. I can't look away from him. I love the way he holds my gaze and seems to be searching my expression.

His eyes slide down my face, and he points to my mouth. "You have . . ."

"What?"

"Blueberry sauce," he says, his voice low and husky.

"I do?"

I swipe the side of my mouth, but he shakes his head. "Missed it."

"Where?"

My eyes follow his hand. He brushes the pad of his thumb over the corner of my lip. My breath catches. His touch lasts less than a second, but it sparks in my chest, a thrilling sensation rushing over my skin. This moment is like a match on kindling, and now I'm lit up. All these months of longing bubble to the surface. I grip the counter, dig my sandals into the floor, and look down.

This is silly. This is foolish. I have a crush on my boss, nothing more. The late hour is playing a trick on me, making me think nighttime is for opportunity.

In reality, midnight is for mistakes.

When I raise my face, Simon is still looking at me. Butterflies race through my body, and I wish for all the things I can't have right now. I wish desperately, wanting a collision with him. His body pressed close. His lips exploring mine. His hands on my arms, my face, my hair.

I want to say something but I don't know where to start, what to whisper, how to even begin to give words to these seconds that seem to hover in a new territory. Our gazes lock, heat flickering between us, a pull that feels magnetic. I hold my breath. If neither one of us says a word, this won't be a foolish risk. If we just stay here, existing in this moment, me searching his face and him studying my eyes, we can pretend there's nothing between us.

But that would be a lie.

This isn't unrequited. It's two-way, hot and electric. Men don't linger in the dark and look at women like this without wanting more. Without wanting them.

A beep breaks the silence. It sounds foreign.

Then it registers. My iPad is beeping.

The noise knocks me into reality. I fumble for the tablet, my fingers slippery as I try to reconnect to the world around us.

"Eagle alert," I whisper, pointing at the device, my pulse still thundering. "I set it to beep when there's activity in the nest."

"This late?"

"You never know." I brush my finger on the screen and check out the nest, lit in infrared, courtesy of the Eagle Cam. But the mama bird is simply adjusting herself, settling into her spot on top of the babies before she turns her head backward and tucks it into her feathers.

Together, we watch the screen. All is quiet now as the eagle lady settles into her slumber, the wind blowing harshly over the sticks and pinecones of her home, high above the ground.

Like this, I'm acutely aware of the space between us. How my shoulder is near his. How a subtle inhale would fill my nostrils with his scent—that clean, woodsy scent that turns me on. How our companionship could flip into something else in a heartbeat. I could turn my face, and our lips would be too close for anything but a kiss.

The mere image of his lips on mine sends a burst of heat flaring inside my chest, spreading like quicksilver all through my veins. I bet his kisses are fantastic. I bet I'd melt from head to toe if I ever felt his tongue slide across mine, his hands glide over my hips, his arms rope around me.

This feels like one of those nights that could too easily tip over into more.

But as that thought crystallizes, another voice inside me speaks up. It tells me to be careful. It tells me to go. I've stayed too late, lingered too long.

I'm on the cusp of a risk I shouldn't take. I need my job too much to tango across this line.

"I should go," I say. "Thanks for the cake."

"Thanks for staying."

"It's my job."

He nods several times, as if he's realizing yes, this is my job. That's why I'm here in his home. To watch over Hayden, not to daydream about the man who pays my bills.

Besides, the job matters. If I lose the work, I don't have a cushion to land on. Some of my friends have trust funds, or still get support from their parents. That's not the case for me. I've been paying my own way post-college. My parents are generous, and they'd help if they could, but they're both still working hard every day—Dad's a bank manager and Mom sells real estate in Phoenix. They're focused on putting my three younger brothers through college. They paid a good chunk of my tuition, but I took out loans for the rest. Sure, I *could* live someplace less pricy, but the best jobs for someone with my language skills are in cities like New York. With some creative housing decisions here and there, I've managed to make New York City work for me. I *need* it to work for me— this city is where I can thrive.

That means it's time to get my head on straight and lasso my heart to keep it in check. I gather my things, and Simon walks me to the door. "I called an UberBLACK for you. It should be waiting downstairs. Black Audi."

My heart hammers at the thoughtful gesture of ordering the highest end car option. Stupid organ.

I've worked late before. Simon often has dinner meetings after his daughter goes to bed, and he always arranges an Uber for me on his account. I half want to assume it means something special, but I also like knowing he's a good guy who just wants to make sure I return home safely and in comfort.

Tonight, though, for the first time, I think he might want me, too.

When I return to my shoebox apartment, wash my face, unclasp my necklace, and settle into bed, I'm not sure if I'm happy or sad about this new revelation. On the one hand, if he didn't look at me the way he did tonight, if he didn't touch my lips with that soft finger, I'd have no choice but to let go of this mess of feelings in me.

On the other hand, attraction may have just become a two-way street, and that's harder to turn away from. Harder to stop replaying.

As I slide under the cool sheets, I imagine his hands moving up my skin. A sigh escapes my lips as the fantasy plays out, and my fingers drift south. Then, they find their way between my legs as I picture him exploring my body, brushing his lips across my shoulder, along my neck, over my lips.

I arch my back as shivers rush through me, radiating from my belly, up my chest. It would be this way with him, I'm sure. This intoxicating, this good.

My breathing quickens along with my pace, and I imagine, and imagine, and imagine how it would feel to have him here, climbing over me. I gasp, and the sound expands into a long, lingering moan as I picture him lowering his hard body against mine.

He slides into me, and I shudder. I feel him move in me, and I reach the edge like that. Then, I fall apart, and it's like flying.

Shuddering, I breathe his name into the dark of the night.

* * *

The next morning, I wake up to a text from him, and you'd be hard-pressed to wipe the grin from my face.

Simon: They're feeding the eaglets breakfast. If you're up, this is your fair warning. You might very well overdose from the cuteness.

I might very well overdose from the swooning, because that was kind of the sweetest text ever.

I click on the Eagle Cam, and a rush of endorphins chases through me as I picture that man on the other side of the park watching the same scene that's unfolding before my eyes.

This attraction is not unrequited.

CHAPTER FIVE

Abby

After the Spanish class I teach that morning at a language school on the Upper West Side, I visit with Harper for lunch at a ramen shop off Amsterdam. She shows me her engagement diamond, and it's as stunning as I would expect, a princess cut set in platinum. She became engaged a few weeks ago, and she and Nick took a trip to Italy to celebrate, so this is the first time I've been able to properly gawk.

"Nick's a keeper," I joke as I stare at her ring.

"He absolutely is. And not just because you got my apartment when I moved in with him," she says with a wink. Her apartment is the deal of the century. It's owned by her parents, and the rent is highway-robbery cheap. I love her and her parents madly for making me their new tenant. It's yet another one of the housing choices that have made New York possible for me.

"I would never joke about true romance when it's given me the cheapest rent in Manhattan," I tease.

"And passing along the world's cheapest rent is the biggest sign of true friendship," Harper says, then she takes a breath and squares her shoulders. "But do you know what the second biggest sign is?"

I shake my head. "Nope. But I bet you're about to tell me."

She sets down her spoon. "Will you be one of my bridesmaids?"

I shriek.

There is no other way to describe my reaction but a full-on, high-pitched scream of excitement. I jump off the stool at the counter and squeeze her. I'm at least half a foot shorter, so I look like a pipsqueak in her arms.

"So is that a yes, Abster?"

I let go, smooth my shirt, and adopt a too-cool-for-school expression. "Maybe. Depends what the dress looks like."

She chuckles. "It's hideous. I've chosen a mint green dress with ruffles and a yellow bodice with puffy sleeves."

I smile like a crazy person. "So I'll look like Easter spat me up. Perfect!"

She elbows me and takes a drink from her tea. "But seriously, I think I'm going to do a basic black. So you can wear it again."

I press my palms together as if in prayer. "Now that is actually the biggest sign of true friendship."

"And since black is hot, you'll look totally hot, so all the single men will throw themselves at you."

I raise both arms in the air. "Let it rain down hot men at Harper's wedding, Lord." I return to the stool. "And the answer is I couldn't be more excited or honored to be your bridesmaid. Now, tell me your wedding plans."

Over noodles, she chatters about her dream wedding, and I savor every little detail. When we leave the shop, she hooks her arm through mine and says, "Your turn. You tell me stuff. Have you met any amazingly witty, bright, kind, and handsome men in your Spanish class? Wait. No. At the park. Have you found the hottest manny in town and are you going to make totally adorable manny-nanny babies called Annie?"

I laugh as we thread our way up the crowded avenue. "Shockingly, the hot, hetero, single manny is like a red panda. Rarely spotted in the wild."

"I love it when you talk zoology." Harper brushes a strand of red hair from her cheek. "What about in one of your classes?"

"Have I met any red pandas there?" I toss back.

She laughs. "Ha. Any hot guys?"

In addition to the Spanish course, I teach a few classes at corporations that are helping their employees learn more language skills for international business, and I've landed more one-on-one tutoring gigs, too. That's a nice supplemental income, even though the nanny gig pays well, too. But this is New York. A gal needs a lot to live here, even when she's scored a sweet deal on an apartment.

We slow at the crosswalk as the light blinks red. "I haven't had time to check out the fresh meat in the classroom," I joke. "Since, you know, I've been trying to teach them to conjugate."

"You know what they say. First, it starts with conjugation. Then it leads to consummation."

I roll my eyes. "You're insane. And relentless."

She rubs her hands together like a movie villain with an evil plan. "But what if one of your students liked you? You'd be the hot teacher, and then you could have a forbidden relationship with a student," she says, whispering salaciously as the warm sun beats down on us. The light changes and we cross.

"Hate to burst your bubble, but I don't think it's forbidden when I teach adults."

She snaps her fingers. "Dammit. What about Simon, then?"

The directness of her question makes me slow my pace. "What about him?" I reply, keeping my tone even. I don't want to reveal that we're bonding over Eagle Cam updates. The tiny birds of prey are the definition of adorable, and I love sharing the eagles with him. But if I tell Harper that we're texting like this, she'll know my heart, and my misplaced feelings will be open for discussion. I'm not sure I'm ready for that.

"Is the job going well?" she asks, tugging my arm so we keep moving.

"He's a great boss. Super laid-back and easygoing, and smart, and we have fun together." And, holy shit, I've said too much. I've pretty much revealed my hand.

Harper nearly skids to a stop outside a diner. The scent of bacon wafts out when a customer opens the door. My friend pokes me in the shoulder and narrows her blue eyes at me. "You *like* him, like him?"

"No," I say, forcing a big laugh to prove how much I absolutely don't feel that way. "Totally not."

She crosses her arms. "Denial will get you nowhere. I can tell."

"How?"

"That fake laugh, for one. As well as that litany of his oh-so-fine-I-wish-he-were-mine traits."

I try to wave it off. "Definitely not," I fire back, but the flush racing across my cheeks makes protesting pointless.

"And now, the color of your cheeks."

"Fine," I say with a grumble. "Maybe I like him a little."

One of her eyebrows rises. "A little?"

"Okay, a lot," I admit.

Her eyes light up. "Called it!"

Relief floods me unexpectedly. It's good to have admitted something I've kept bottled up for so long. Maybe I do want to discuss him. Oh hell, do I ever want to talk about him. "Do you think it's ridiculous to have a thing for my boss?" I hold up a hand as a stop sign. "Wait. Don't answer. I already know. It is beyond ridiculous."

She drapes her arm around me. "I don't think it's ridiculous at all. He's a good guy, he's crazy about his kid, and he takes her around the city doing cool things with her. But you know that better than I do. What I know is he was *determined* last fall to find someone who would *also* do all those cool things with Hayden. Someone who would be engaged in the Natural History Museum when she took Hayden, not in texting her other nanny friends about what to do after work. That's why I hooked him up with you. And I know the job is important to you, too, so whatever happens just be careful, okay? That's all."

"You mean be sure to use protection?" I say with a straight face.

Her eyes nearly pop out. "Not exactly what I meant. But, duh. Yes. Obviously." She pauses, then adopts a serious tone. "But I meant with your heart and your head."

"I know," I say softly.

"There's a lot at stake. That's why I say it."

I sigh. "Yeah, you're right. I'll be careful, I promise."

She points at me. "I'll see you Friday right. We're still going out?"

I nod. "Of course. Text me the time."

She gives me a quick hug then takes off.

I repeat her warning as I walk across town to Simon's gorgeous home on the Upper East side.

Be careful.

I'm careful as I reach his building and step into the elevator. As I press my hand on my belly, I'm careful to quiet the riot of excitement in my body. I'm careful as I reach his floor and knock on the door, wild nerves thrumming through me.

Hayden opens the door, swinging it wide. She hugs my waist, nearly tackling me. "Abby! Come join the tea party!"

She grabs my hand and tugs me into the living room, gesturing grandly to her sky-blue kid-size table with dinosaur designs on it. It's set for tea, and her father is enjoying a cup.

I try desperately not to think of him touching my face last night. Or sending me texts this morning. Or bringing me cake.

But the battle is lost. How could I think anything but sweet, dizzying thoughts when I set eyes on him? The man is utterly adorable at the little table, his knees up high since he's parked in a tiny chair, having a tea party with his daughter and her stuffed elephant.

Hayden grabs her chair and pats the extra one for me. I drop my bag, smile at Simon, and slide right in to the party. I fit much better at this table than he does.

"Would you like more peach raspberry chocolate coconut tea?" Hayden asks the elephant.

Simon picks up the gray stuffed animal and makes him nod. "Why, yes please. With honey and sugar and syrup," he says in a deep voice.

Hayden lifts her plastic teapot and pours for the stuffed animal. She holds up the pot and looks at me. "Would you like some of this special magical potion tea?"

I nod enthusiastically. "I would love some. What does the magical potion tea do?"

She stage-whispers as she pours, "It turns your hair purple."

My eyes become moons, and I clap. "I came to the right tea party. I've been looking for a tea to do just that!"

She hands me the cup and I take an imaginary gulp. I run my hand over my wavy hair, and Simon pretends to be astonished. "It's happening already. I can see the shades of violet starting."

Hayden shoots him a *you're-so-wrong* look. "No, Daddy. It turns out she accidentally drank the rainbow potion tea, and once your hair turns into a rainbow, the leprechauns will steal you away." She snaps her gaze to me. "Abby! Your hair is turning all the colors in the rainbow."

I drop my mouth into an *O*. "Will it be like this forever?" I dart my eyes around, as if searching for the little men. "Are they going to come get me?"

Hayden pours more pretend tea in a jiffy. "Not if you drink the antidote quickly," she says, and thrusts a cup at me.

I down it in a sliver of a second. "Is my hair back to normal?"

"It's all better," she declares, a bright smile on her face.

"Whew." Simon wipes his hand over his brow. "We almost lost Abby to the leprechauns."

"I'm so glad we were able to save her," Hayden echoes, with the intense make-believe relief of a five-year-old.

Hayden proceeds to serve us purple and black cookies (pretend), then neon cake (also imaginary), and finally an electric biscuit (also not real). They're all exceedingly delicious.

"What was your favorite of the treats?" she asks her father.

"Definitely the electric biscuit," he answers.

"Can you get it on the menu at Gabriel's?"

"I will do my very best to discuss it with him."

I smile at their conversation, and her interpretation of his job. They have such a great relationship. That's how it should be, yet the ease of their chatting and playing is rare. It's a testament to him and how much of himself he gives to being a dad.

While I'm not keen to have kids anytime soon, the fact that Simon is such a good father . . . well, I'll just say it. It's a massive turn-on. When I watch him interact with his daughter, it's as if I'm overdosing on some basic, human female-to-male attraction. Simon isn't one of those sitcom dads who's a total buffoon and freaks out when his daughter has to pee, or take a bath, or put on a dress. He's not the single dad who hired the nanny because he can't figure out how to parent.

He's the opposite. He's completely capable. He hired me because he's busy with work, not because he's one of those idiot fathers who forgets to pick up his kid from daycare, like in a slapstick comedy, and then races all over town to face the stern, disapproving glare of the daycare owner. Simon is the opposite. He knows how to take his daughter to the doctor, how to care for her when she has a fever, and how to shop for clothes.

My God, the man even knows how to braid her hair.

Well, regular braid. Not French braid. That may be his Achilles' heel.

A few weeks ago, I told Hayden that going to bed in braids was a sure-fire way to wake up with curly hair. She likes my curls and waves, so she'd begged him to style her hair that way. While I'd like to say I taught him how, he already knew a basic braid. But when Hayden had asked for a French braid the next night, he'd turned to me with a helpless shrug. "Any chance you can show me how to French braid my daughter's hair?"

He'd had this sweet lopsided grin, and a hopeful look in his light blue eyes that made it impossible to resist.

"Why, I thought you'd never ask." I'd showed him how to French braid, and, okay, fine, maybe he had been a bit sitcom dad then. He hadn't been able to master it, no matter how hard he tried. Hayden's hair had been a crisscrossed mess, and I'd had to come to the rescue and style it.

So there's one thing he's no good at. No one's perfect.

Hayden finishes her last pretend cookie then taps my arm. "Abby, can we go to the park today and play soccer?"

"Absolutely," I say, as we rise from the table and straighten up the tea party.

Simon gestures to his dress shirt and slacks, almost apologetically. "I should go. Meetings and all."

He keeps unusual hours, but they work for us. Since he's often out late at dinners, he's usually around in the morning to take Hayden to school or classes. Now that it's summer, he spends the mornings with her, and I don't come in most days until after twelve. That's good for me because it gives me plenty of time for my tutoring and teaching in the mornings.

After a quick hug with Hayden, he says goodbye and takes off, the door clicking shut behind him.

I breathe a deep sigh of relief when he's gone. I'd expected today to be awkward, given the rampage of butterflies in my chest when I arrived. But evidently, last night was a mere blip, one of those moments where there's energy and connection, but nothing comes of it. Fine by me. We might have a little spark, but that doesn't mean we'll necessarily catch fire.

I spend the day with Hayden: kicking a soccer ball in the park, chasing her around the playground, then we ride the merry-go-round, and finally we stop at a food truck and snag hummus and pitas and bottled waters for dinner, relaxing on a park bench as we chat about the clouds and the sky and the trees.

When we return to her house in the early evening, I run a bath for her, then make sure to brush my teeth. It's always good to brush after meals, right? Especially after eating hummus. I'm not doing it because I want fresh breath for her dad when he returns home in a few minutes.

Even if that flutter in my chest when I hear the door unlock threatens to give me away.

CHAPTER SIX

Simon

Hayden crashes in seconds. It's her special skill, falling asleep instantly once she hits the covers. The clock reads a little past eight, and I should let Abby go, but I want to snag a few minutes with her to catch up on their day. One of my favorite parts of working with her is hearing her recap what they did, and what Hayden learned and enjoyed that day, from new Spanish words and sayings to fresh interests and dislikes.

But as I head into the living room where Abby's packing up her purse, my phone bleats. I glance at the screen. It's Gabriel's business manager, Eduardo. I answer, holding up a finger to let Abby know I'll be fast, and I want to chat with her.

She settles into the couch and flips on her iPad. On the phone, I rattle off some of the details Eduardo is looking for, and out of the corner of my eye, I see Abby toggle over to the Eagle Cam. Her face lights up when she flicks to an earlier shot of the mother eagle watching over the eaglets as they practice standing up on their wobbly, fluffy frames.

I walk behind the couch and lean closer, watching the little birds practice being bigger birds.

Baby eagles are covered in tufts of gray feathers. They don't take on the iconic brown body and white head of the nation's symbol until they're older than four; I've learned that from my eagle research. But already their talons are huge. It's a funny sight, the bird of prey equivalent to a puppy dog with humongous paws. I imitate a loping dog, and Abby laughs quietly.

Then, Gabriel's guy asks me a question, half in English, half in French. I know enough French to be dangerous, so I fire off a response, suggesting we develop a plan tomorrow.

Abby whips her head around and stares slack-jawed at me.

What? I mouth.

She blinks, shakes her head, and whispers, "You just asked if he wants to swim naked in the summer."

Oh shit.

"*Je suis désolé.*" I apologize to Eduardo, who's laughing.

"That is okay. I prefer to swim naked with a woman," he says drily.

"As do I," I add.

After a few more minutes of awkward conversation, since he doesn't seem to like speaking English, and I'm, evidently, far too dangerous when I attempt French, we agree to reconnect tomorrow. When I hang up, I flop on the second couch, across from Abby. Her lips are quirked up as if she's waiting to chuckle.

I hold my arms out wide. "What? In most circumstances, swimming naked is fun," I say, like I can justify my faux pas.

She launches a couch pillow in my general direction. I catch it in one hand.

"But not with someone you're doing a business deal with," she says, laughing.

"Fine. You may be right there." I sit up and run my hand across the back of my neck. "So you speak French, too?"

"*Oui.*"

That both surprises me, and doesn't at all. "I knew you spoke Spanish and German, along with Mandarin, and that you're learning Italian, but I didn't know you spoke French. You just said you were learning it," I say, since we talked about her language fluency in the job interview.

She shrugs and smiles, like a little elf. "I *was* learning it then. Now I've learned it."

My jaw drops. "Learned it? In seven months?"

She nods. "I had a good base of knowledge from high school and college. I did some online tutorials, practiced with an app, and boom. Now I know it."

"That's all it took?"

She nods proudly. "I picked it up super fast."

"That's cheetah speed."

She beams. "It's my party trick. Learning new languages, lickety-split. My mom is Spanish and my dad is—"

I jump in. "German." She smiles wide and nods. "I knew that about your parents. You've told me before." I don't want her to think I've forgotten a basic detail. Women like good listeners. I happen to have awesome ears, and it can't hurt for her to know how well they work.

She fluffs out her blond hair. "Hair color from Dad." She gestures to her hazel eyes, making a *V* over them with her fingers. "Eyes from Mom." Then she gazes upward, as if she's staring at something tall. "Height, though? No idea where that little bitty thing came from." She shrugs. "Both my parents are giants, and I topped out at five-two. But you know what's great about being short?"

"Tell me," I say, settling into the couch, loving that we're just . . . chatting. Besides, she's more than a foot shorter than me, so I don't have a clue what she's about to say.

She counts off on her fingers. "For starters, plenty of legroom on planes. Plus, I'm always getting carded, which is totally flattering, and I can also wear any height heels I want. And, some large shirts can double as dresses."

The last one cracks me up. Then she says something rapid-fire in French. I furrow my brow. She quickly translates. "Good things come in small packages."

Oh, how I want to make a flirty comment about her being a good thing, or a dirty comment about big packages, and maybe even something filthier about . . . coming. Instead, I zoom back to languages. "Even for you, that's quick to learn French, though. It took me several years in school to learn it."

She takes a breath as she points at me. "Um, Simon. I hate to break it to you, but I don't think you know French."

I heave a sigh and drag a hand through my hair. "Guess I'm rustier than I thought. I get the feeling Gabriel's guys would be more keen if I could speak better French."

She raises an eyebrow. "You really think it would make a difference in the deal?"

I tilt my head, considering her question, then I nod. "I do, because it would impress them. Make me stand out. It would show them a commitment to their particular brand of . . ." I'm about to say *cuisine*, but instead, I opt for, "their brand of *je ne sais quoi*."

She flashes an appreciative grin then leans forward. "Would you like me to help you?"

More time with Abby? I barely have to think on that one, but I pretend to contemplate, stroking my chin. "Hmm. Well, let's see. I'm terrible. You're good. That's a no-brainer."

"Good. I love teaching. I'm excited to help you."

I can't even begin to explain how excited I am to be her student. But I've got to keep that to myself. I focus on the details instead. "But I insist on paying you."

She scoffs. "I insist on not taking your money."

"You can't teach me for free."

"Don't think of it as free. It helps me to work on my language teaching skills. Fair trade?"

Deal-making is my stock-in-trade, so I press on. "I'd really like to pay you, though. I value your time, Abby."

She shoots me a smile. "I know you do. But the offer is only for free, not for pay." She arches an eyebrow playfully. "Take it or leave it."

I shake my head, impressed with her negotiation skills and how she's bested me. "You're quite the deal-maker."

"I drive a hard bargain," she jokes.

You absolutely fucking do. "Yes. Very hard," I say, teasing, even though in some ways I'm not teasing at all.

"Want to start tonight?" She sounds eager.

"You don't have anywhere to be?" I ask. Then, because I can't help myself, I toss out, "Like a hot date?"

It's borderline ridiculous how I'm fishing for information, but my need to know outweighs my wish to be nonchalant. Besides, I threw in the towel on the pursuit of cool when I had a kid. Dads aren't expected to be cool. Ergo, I can fish.

She laughs loudly. "No hot date tonight. Nor yesterday. Nor tomorrow."

A smile tugs at my lips, then it spreads wider when she adds, "And not the next night, either."

And that, ladies and gentlemen, is news worth prying for. Abby is thoroughly single, and I pump a virtual fist.

Not that I'm going to ask her on a date. But hell, if I can't have her, no one else should. Yeah, I know that sounds unfair and possessive. So be it. I have a caveman inside of me. I might hide him most of the time under the crisp shirts in my Upper East Side lair, but he's here, and I don't want anyone else to get his hands on this woman.

"Good," I say, before I can I catch myself.

We spend the next hour on the couch, and I can't complain at all about my life at the moment. Just being near her is like a shot of endorphins. Add in the fact that she's patient, fun, and focused as we work on French, and I'm a happy camper. Plus, I've learned a few new phrases, including how to correctly pronounce what I'd intended to ask Eduardo. *Do you want to develop a new plan tomorrow?*

"*Voulez-vous aménager un nouveau plan demain?*" I say, and Abby smiles and claps softly.

"*Très bien,*" she says, her lips curving up. "Or use *développer* instead of *aménager*. Overall, either is much better than *voulez-vous nager nu dans l'été*." She repeats my initial attempt, saying it the way I did, with the pronunciation so off that my question turned into a big gaffe.

I flub my lips and hold out my hands. "What can you do?"

"No more skinny-dipping invitations," she says, wagging her finger. "Besides, skinny-dipping is way overrated."

My ears perk. So does another part, which sits up and takes notice as she talks about nudity. "What makes you say that?"

"Because . . . water."

I frown in confusion. "You don't like water?"

She laughs. "I assure you, I adore water. I just think that the role of it in, you know . . ." Her tone suddenly becomes shy.

"Foreplay?" I supply, and I really shouldn't go here. But I'm doing it anyway.

She blushes. "Yes, that."

"So skinny-dipping as foreplay is overrated? And why is that?" I ask, because she went there and I'm absolutely following her.

She raises her chin, no longer shy as she says, "Because water is not a lubricant."

My eyebrows shoot into my hairline. Abby has a dirty mind. Abby has a naughty side. Holy hell, I want to get to know this side of her so much. "You're probably right on that count. But there are other ways to get wet in the water," I say, before I let good judgment wrest control of my mouth again. And I better regain control before I fucking flirt straight into the land of filthy innuendo, because I don't know if I can return from it, or if I want to.

"I have no doubt there are better ways," she says with a naughty grin, and there's something teasingly seductive in her tone that makes me think she likes this tango, too. I'd like to go back in time and thank the me from an hour ago for incorrectly using the French verb for swim on a business call.

"But if skinny-dipping is overrated, are showers, too?" There's more gravel in my voice than before. She has to hear it. She has to be aware of this game we're playing.

She nibbles on the corner of her bottom lip. "I think showers and certain activities in them would have a top-notch rating," she says, her eyes locked on mine. My blood heats, and there's no way I can contemplate anything but the images flying through my mind. Her, in my shower, water streaking along her bare skin. Me, joining her under the steam, pressing her hands to the wall, angling her hips just so. Then having my way with her.

"I think so, too," I rasp, and a handful of words I want to add to my statement dances dangerously on the tip of my tongue.

With you.

Now.

Let's test this theory.

I swallow roughly, far too tempted to say something suggestive. Somehow, I grab a lifeline and pull myself up from the slippery slope. "And *merci*. I'm thankful for the lesson," I say in French.

That does the trick. Forcing my brain to translate has knocked me back into reality.

She returns seamlessly, too. "Very good. Your language skills are better than your French-braiding skills," she teases as she shuts her iPad.

I pretend to be insulted. "So not true. I can do French braids with my eyes closed."

She shakes her head. "Somehow, I doubt that."

"I'll prove it to you."

She tilts her head, and her hand freezes on her purse. "Prove it?" she asks quietly.

Somehow I've thrown a gauntlet I didn't realize I was tossing. I do the only natural next thing—follow through. "Sure. Got one of those hair tie things?"

She nods slowly. "Yes, but . . ." Her voice trails off. Then she resumes the thought. "You really learned to French braid?"

I nod. "Hayden insisted on it," I explain then study her face. Her pupils are dilated, and she blinks. Ah hell, I've made her wary with my remark. "I don't have to prove it. I was just teasing," I say, giving her an out. Mildly flirty comments are one thing—hands in hair are another.

A small grin spreads on her face, as she dips her hand into her purse and produces a black elastic band. "No, I insist. You were horrible last time. Have at it."

She drops to the floor, scoots over to me, and with her shoulder, she nudges my right knee.

Hello, slippery slope. Funny to see you again so soon.

CHAPTER SEVEN

Simon

Her other shoulder bumps my other knee. There's no need to think—I widen my legs more and let her settle in between them. I'm seated on the couch, she's on the floor, and she waits for me to braid her hair.

As I stare at her lush, blond locks, the breath escapes my lungs. For a moment, it's as if I'm hovering in a state of suspended want. Like this is the real line we're crossing. Not me bringing her dessert, or touching the corner of her lips, or gazing at her face longer than I should. Not even sending texts about a pair of wild birds or making comments about showers and nudity.

But *this*.

Touching her hair.

Fuck, I love her hair.

I slide the tie over my wrist, then gather up some strands near the top of her head. "Confession," I say in a quiet voice. "I watched a few YouTube videos after you taught me."

She leans back, and I can feel her smile. "Like I said, prove it."

"It's on." I focus on the task of separating her honey-blond hair into three sections, running my fingers through them like a comb. I lift the first strand and lay it over the middle one, then the left, gathering more hair into the next section.

After I failed at her first French braid lesson, I took it upon myself to learn. I don't like not being able to master basic skills. A man should be able to braid his daughter's hair.

And his woman's hair.

"How does it look?" Her voice sounds a little breathy.

"Like it was braided by a man who learned by watching YouTube videos," I answer.

She laughs lightly and leans into me more, inching closer. My hands still for a moment. I feel like I'm in high school again. Like I have a crush on a girl, and I don't know what to do, where to go next, what to say.

The thing is, I *do* know. I just don't know that I *should*. But I know what I want. There's no doubt in my mind. I want to touch her, to kiss her, to feel her body press against mine. Even the chance to touch her like this is intoxicating, a rush of blood to the head. Her waves of hair are soft, and they feel spectacular falling through my fingers. I can't picture a single thing besides running my hands through these strands as I kiss her, as I touch her, as she moves beneath me.

Just like that, I imagine her in bed.

Yeah, it's not the first time. It's not the hundredth, either. I've pictured this countless fucking times, but it's a fantastic image. Her softness, her sweetness, her curves. I see her mouth falling open, her breath coming fast, her arms roped around me. I blink, trying to eradicate these images from my mind, but I've no doubt they'll return later when she's gone and I'm alone under the sheets.

I continue the braid, trying my best to focus on the simple task as I move farther down her hair. I keep my eyes trained on the weave, one after the other, as if the act of braiding can erase all these other thoughts. She bends her head, exposing more of her neck, and I exhale hard.

"Fuck," I mutter.

She tenses. "Is everything okay?"

I close my eyes, stopping my moves, reeling in my desire. "Yeah. You just . . ."

I stop myself. I can't go there. Can't say this. Can't do this. But my God, I dream about kissing her neck. I want to smother her neck in kisses, brush my lips over her skin, and feel her melt against me. I want to do things to her that make her knees weak and her panties damp.

"Just what?" she asks, her voice small, but desperate, as if she wants the answer as badly as I want to give it. The possibility that she feels the same sends a charge through me.

"You just have nice hair," I whisper, then I want to kick myself.

You have nice hair? I mouth, grateful she can't see me.

"So do you," she says. A wave of heat crashes into me, and I let it lead me on. Let it pull me closer. Let it be the force that bends my face close. I bring my nose to her locks, inches away, and I inhale. The heat turns to fire, twisting and curling in my veins.

"Smells good, too," I say, my voice husky. "Like coconut or something."

"My shampoo," she answers, her voice a bare whisper in the quiet of my home. "You like it?"

My throat is dry. I swallow thickly. Answer truthfully. "I love it."

I weave the remaining strands, grab the tie, and loop it around the end, finishing the job.

"How does it look?"

I run my index finger along the French braid, tight against her head. "I'd never be mistaken for a hair stylist, but I think it's safe to say I can braid French better than I can speak it," I say, going for self-deprecating humor. Laughing lightly, she raises her hands and runs her fingers along my handiwork.

My eyes roam along her arms, her bare skin on display in her peach tank top.

In this moment, I am a dirty old man, because all I want to do is take this twenty-six-year-old woman and have her as mine. I want to run my hands along her arms, lift her up, turn her around, and bring her down on my lap, telling her to straddle me. Then I would kiss the hell out of her. Learn how her lips feel, how her mouth tastes, if she's as soft as I've imagined. If she melts into my arms the way I picture. I want to strip her naked and have my wicked way with her.

I draw a deep breath, and my traitorous hand takes over as I cover hers where it rests against her hair.

She gasps—a surprised, sexy little sound.

I guide her fingers softly over the braid, as if all I'm doing is showing her that I pulled it off. As if I'm not trying desperately to find a way to touch her without letting on how much I want to touch her everywhere. How much I want more of her. All of her.

My skin heats one million degrees as I curl my fingers over hers, bringing our joined hands along her soft hair. I swear she's holding her breath as we travel over the braid, and her reaction emboldens me. My fingertips brush the edge of her cheekbone. I'm taking chances left and right—chances I shouldn't take. But I don't want to stop.

She inhales sharply, and just as I'm about to knock some sense into my wandering fingers, she leans farther back into me and whispers, "Yes, you do know how to braid hair now."

My home is so quiet, I swear I can hear the vibrations between us in the air, humming faintly with possibility, like the moment before a storm when you can sense that the sky is about to burst open. I'm confident she feels it, too. I sense it in her shoulders against my legs, her breathy voice, her words.

I can barely stand it anymore. The tension tightens, and soon it's going to snap. Being this close to her and not taking her in my arms is insanity. I want to ask her what she's thinking and if this feeling is as mutual as it seems with her between my legs and my hands in her hair.

"Abby . . ." I say, but then I cut myself off.

Soft footsteps pad against hardwood.

I yank my hand away, and Abby scoots forward in a flurry. My heart hammers madly, and my skin prickles as I back up into the couch cushions, putting distance between us.

But Hayden doesn't even wander into the living room. The faint sound of water running tells me she simply got a cup of water in the bathroom.

Still, my pulse thunders as if I've been caught stealing, and by my own kid.

I stand. "Better go check on her." I stride across the living room and down the hall, poking my head into my little girl's room. She slides back under the covers.

A faint, sleepy smile spreads on her face. "Night, Daddy."

"Night, sweetie," I say, and tug her purple blanket up higher. She'll kick it off in the middle of the night. But I cover her anyway then drop a kiss to her warm cheek.

I turn away from her bed, drag a hand through my hair, and take a breath, letting it spread through me. I remind myself I've done nothing wrong. I've crossed no lines. But my heart pounds relentlessly, so I press my palm against the doorframe and will my pulse to settle down.

Thirty seconds later, I return to the living room.

Abby stands, slings her bag onto her shoulder, smooths her top, and flashes a too-bright smile. The moment has vanished, and all that wild possibility is not just drained away—it's erased.

An empty sensation takes root in my chest, but then I tell myself this is for the best. I shouldn't have my hands on my kid's nanny. Shouldn't flirt. Shouldn't braid her hair. I need her in Hayden's life too much. I can't risk that simply because I want her so fucking much. My longing for her shouldn't occupy its own damn zip code.

It's becoming really inconvenient.

"It's late. I should go," she says softly, a sweet smile pulling at her lips.

I nod.

"But let me know if you want to work on French again," she adds, and it's as if she's tossing me a rope.

I want to be a good guy who doesn't cross lines he shouldn't. I'd like to be the guy who can walk away from her offer.

But I need to improve my skills. Hell, if I don't learn a few more words, then the next time I try to speak in French, I'll be asking Gabriel if he wants to cartwheel in combat boots or eat whipped cream off a steak. That's enough for me to grab the end of the rope. I nod in Hayden's direction. "She's with her mom the next few days," I say, even though Abby knows this, since she's off.

Her tone is upbeat as she says, "Let's teach you French, then."

I'm about to ask when she wants to meet, but she's faster. "Maybe we can meet at a coffee shop? Or the library?"

That's as good an answer as anything. It tells me all I need to know. We're not meeting *here*. Lord knows, we've done enough here tonight. It's too dangerous. It's the fire zone, and if we take another step, someone will get burned.

We'll be safe out of my home. "Sounds like a plan." Then I grin and repeat it in French.

She smiles, her eyes twinkling, as she says "*Très bien.*"

I walk her to the door and hold it open for her. "Goodnight, Abby." My voice is quieter than usual, but rougher, too.

She looks at me, parts her lips as if she wants to say something more, but then she simply swallows and says, "Goodnight, Simon."

And hell, if that soft, sweet voice of hers doesn't stir up my desire for her once more.

But I shove it away.

When she walks down the hall, her hair falls in curls along her back. She undid the braid, and I miss seeing it more than I should.

CHAPTER EIGHT

Abby

I take my first ever cold shower that night.

I shiver under the water, and the chill seeps into my bones. My teeth chatter, and I'm dying to jack up the hot water and let it rain over me.

I resist.

I stay under the frigid stream, determined to win this battle with my lust.

Soon enough, the coldness gobbles up all the red-hot desire in me.

The Antarctica strategy worked. I'm officially a popsicle, but I've achieved my goal.

I'm 100 percent turned off.

With my tundra hands, I shut off the faucet, dry off, then wrap myself in a fluffy towel. When I'm done, I pull on a blue college T-shirt from one of my brothers and grab a pair of white underwear. Not the pretty lacy kind. The *ugly* cotton kind. The *on-my-period* kind. It's not shark week, but my mission is sex repellent. Rooting through my drawers, I grab an old pair of workout pants, too.

God, these gray sweats are hideous. I don't even know why I own them.

I cinch the drawstring tight and give my fingers the evil eye. Especially the index finger, that busy bitch.

Don't go there. Don't even think about dipping below the belt.

Returning to the world's tiniest bathroom, I yank open the medicine cabinet and snag a tube of face mask. Spreading it all over my forehead, nose, and cheeks is like applying frosting on an anti-lust cake. I'm covered in light blue goop that smells faintly of tofu and lemon. Quite possibly, I'm approaching revolting levels.

Excellent.

Closing the tube, I appraise myself in the mirror. My handiwork is astonishingly effective. I'm chilled like a seafood salad, I look like the newest member of Blue Man Group, I smell like a vegan café, and I'm dressed like my brother.

Mission more than accomplished.

My own hand doesn't even want to get it on with the girl in the mirror. That's a victory, considering what my favorite late-night activity for the last several weeks has been —getting off to fantasies of Simon. I have a lovely series of go-to gifs in my brain featuring that very subject.

Not tonight, though.

When I slip under the blanket, I grab my iPad and consider practicing Italian. But that language is far too alluring. It'll lead me back to him. Sliding my thumb over my eReader shelves, I quickly decide that's no better, given the array of romance novels mixed in with my language books.

I click over to Pinterest and, on a whim, decide to look up images of yellow raincoats, since that's not sensual at all. I see kids in wellies, twirling polka-dot umbrellas, and small dogs wearing jackets while the sky pours, and I've definitely proved my own theory. Water's not a lubricant at all.

My hands stay above my waistline. Yay me. I've succeeded in the Refrain from Finger-Painting While Imagining Your Boss event at the Sexual Abstinence Olympics.

"Gold medal for Abby," I mutter, then I drift off. When I wake up, my pillowcase is caked with blue sludge, but I survived the night without diddling.

I tell myself that it's a new day and nothing naughty will happen when I meet Simon at one in the afternoon.

I say it over and over again that morning as I go for a bike ride in Central Park for exercise (since I am convinced running was invented as a form of torture). I tell myself again as I head to a Spanish tutoring session at a management consultant's office, and then as I take the subway downtown.

I repeat it one more time as I arrive at Café Gitane in NoLita, a tiny, casual restaurant that serves French Moroccan dishes. But I'm jittery inside, as if I've had far too much caffeine. The nervousness courses through me, because last night we teetered on the precipice, so close to caving. I've no clue what to expect today or if the cold shower therapy lasts longer than twelve hours. Maybe I should have taken another dose this morning, because I don't know how I'll feel when I see him.

The answer arrives in a heartbeat when I turn around. He walks toward me. Ten feet away, and my pulse quickens. Five feet, and my throat is dry. Two feet, and my stomach pirouettes.

Simon is scrumptious in his jeans and light-blue, short-sleeved button-down that shows off his arms, roped with muscles. I would say I'm an arms girl, but I'm actually an everything girl. Give me strong arms, a firm butt, a nice set of abs, muscular legs, a great face, soulful eyes, soft hair, and a beautiful heart.

I want it all.

Nothing wrong with that.

He has it all.

"Hi, Simon," I say, and I'm impressed I said those two words without climbing him like a tree. *I can do this. I'm a rock star at resisting.*

"Hi Abby." His lips curve up in a grin. "Should we grab a table?"

"We can grab a table or we can sit at one," I say with a goofy smile. It's a terrible joke. But hey, whatever works, right?

"I'll opt for sitting," he says, and we pick a table on the sidewalk.

He pulls out a chair for me. That's another point in his favor—he's polite. But I already knew he was a gentleman. I stand no chance.

"Thanks," I say, sitting down, willing the organ in my chest to stop beating in overtime. Nothing naughty can happen at one in the afternoon.

The sun is bright, the sky is blue, and we're nowhere close to alone. *Good.* Sitting outside is the perfect antidote to last night. It's protection from all those devilish hormones that threatened to derail me in the dark of his home. Here in the light of day, surrounded by New Yorkers scurrying along the sidewalk, I won't be tempted. Even though he looks so damn handsome.

"I thought this would be the perfect spot to work on your French," I say, spreading the napkin over my lap.

"I've heard great things about this place but haven't had the chance to try it, so all the better. The avocado toast is supposed to be quite good, and so is the couscous with red peppers and toasted pine nuts," he says, and I breathe a sigh of relief, because picking what to eat is now one less thing I have to think about.

Fighting off the desire to throw myself at him is hard enough. Add in trying to order food and my brain would short-circuit.

"Let's get that," I say. After we order, the redheaded waiter asks if we want wine.

Simon meets my eyes. "Glass of white?"

God, yes. A whole bottle please, and a funnel so I can down it quickly. "That sounds perfect."

The waiter clears his throat and asks quietly, "Could I trouble you for your ID?"

Simon cracks up, looking away from me and covering his mouth. I laugh, too. "Told you so," I say, then dip into my purse and flash my license at the waiter.

The guy reads it, then smiles. "You look young, and I mean that as a compliment."

"I'm guessing you don't want to see mine," Simon deadpans to the waiter.

A faint blush creeps across the guy's pale cheeks. "Um," he stammers. "If you'd like to show it to me. But it's not necessary, sir."

Simon shakes his head, laughing. "We're all good," he says, and the guy walks off.

"And to think, having a drink with *you* didn't even age *me* up in his eyes."

Then it hits me, what I just said. I'm having a drink with Simon. I've never had a drink with him before, since I've been with his daughter every other time I've seen him.

This is the first time we've been together like this outside of his home, sans Hayden.

The realization hits me hard.

This is a first time.

We're at a restaurant.

At a table for two.

Try as I might to rationalize that one in the afternoon is an innocent time on the clock, when I take in the two of us at a sidewalk table, ordering wine and food, this feels distinctly like . . .

Nope.

Won't go there.

Can't go there.

Because nothing naughty can happen now . . . not with me drinking wine, and him looking gorgeous, and us far away from his home.

Uh-oh.

This has all the ingredients for a perfect dish of temptation.

I force myself to catalogue this hour with him as one-on-one language tutoring, not a date with the man I long for.

I break out my iPad, click on my French notes, and say, "Let's get started."

He nods and flashes me the smile of his that shows off his straight white teeth. His eyes lock briefly with mine. "Tutor me, Abby," he says, and my stomach executes a loop-de-loop, because he just made those three words sound sexy.

I'm a teacher who wants the student, and I am so screwed.

CHAPTER NINE

Abby

An hour later, he's learned several new key terms to use in his conversations with Gabriel's business manager, and we've practiced other phrases that will be helpful to him, too, like "terms of the contract," and "return on investment."

"You're a fast learner," I say, and it's true. While I don't expect him to be holding entire conversations, he's picking up new words quickly. "You definitely have a good base of knowledge."

"Thank you. And I have a good teacher," he says and raises his glass of wine, clinking it with mine. "Here's to not inviting business partners to swim naked."

"Exactly. My goal is no more verbal blunders for you," I say with a smile, doing my best to keep it light.

He finishes his glass and sets it down. "That is an admirable goal. How many more lessons do you think I need to achieve that?"

Endless. As many as we can possibly arrange, because this last hour eating, and drinking, and dining, and talking has felt exactly like a date.

Oops. I went there.

I take another swallow from my second glass of wine. The drink has helped calm my jitters and so has the focus on French. "A few more," I say with a jut of my shoulder.

Crap. That was a flirty move. *Must. Rein. In. Desire. To. Launch. Self. At. Simon.*

He leans back in his chair. "Then we should plan a tour of all the off-the-beaten-path French cafés and restaurants for our tutoring lessons." He sweeps his hand out wide, as if he's showing off a billboard. "Food and language."

Yes, that sounds perfect. Take me out for delicious meals and let me teach you how to speak a fucking sexy language, because you sound so hot saying "terms of the contract" in French.

"That sounds like a fantastic plan," I say, crossing my legs and hunting for a new topic that will be safer than this chatter about what the two of us will do. "So how did you get into the restaurant business? Were you just fed up with Wall Street?"

He hums then answers, "I had a good run in finance, but it's a soulless business, and a potentially obsessive one, too. I wanted to get out before I became soulless and obsessive, too."

"Were you starting to?"

"I was on the path, veering in that direction. I worked too many late nights. Definitely before Hayden was born." He sighs heavily, and his voice is tinged with regret.

"Maybe even after," he says, as if he's admitting something difficult.

"Were you a workaholic?"

He shrugs and quirks his lips. Briefly, he looks away. "I was called that."

He doesn't have to speak the words aloud for me to know *who* called him that. His ex-wife. My chest pinches painfully, and I wish he didn't have an ex-wife. That I could wave a magic wand and she'd simply vanish into thin air. That's a terribly unfair thing to wish, for Hayden's sake. But even so, it's what I feel—the desire to erase his history. To take away the hurt she inflicted on him. But then, his hurt brought him into my life. It's part of who he is—the single father, doing most of the work raising his daughter.

I run my finger along the edge of my glass then meet Simon's eyes. "Do you think you are now? A workaholic?"

His gaze locks with mine. "Do you?" His question is laced with worry, and I can tell he desperately hopes I'll say no.

Saying no is easy, though, because it's the truth. The man works hard, but I don't think he's dangerously addicted to it. A reassuring smile tugs at my lips. "No. You're not a workaholic at all. I also think you're a great father to Hayden."

He matches my grin with one of his own. "I can't tell you how much I love hearing that."

"Watching the two of you warms my heart. It's the sweetest thing in the world to see you together. You're crazy for her, and she adores you so." He can't stop grinning, and then he lowers his eyes, but the smile remains. "Did I embarrass you by saying that?"

He raises his chin and shakes his head. His blue eyes sparkle. "No. You didn't embarrass me. You made me happy."

Oh God. Oh hell. My heart pounds wildly, the relentless beating a reminder of how utterly foolish I am. It's one thing to banish thoughts of sex, but talking about the things that endear him to me? That's far riskier, because now my heart is swinging back into the zone of longing. This conversation has become just as risky as picturing him unbuttoning his shirt for me.

And now I'm thinking about Simon undressing. Great. Before I drool on the table, I slam on the mental brakes and swerve the car in the other direction. *Work, work, work.* "Tell me then—if finance was soulless, is the restaurant business full of soul?"

He runs a hand through his thick hair and smiles that wide, beaming grin that I adore. "Definitely. Great food ultimately needs to be made with both heart and soul, don't you think?"

"I haven't thought about it before, but that makes sense, I suppose."

"Food is a sensory experience. It can be sensual, and it should be delicious, right?" he asks, his eyes locked on mine.

My skin tingles from his intensity. So much for his career being a safer topic. "Of course. Like the lunch we just had. That was fantastic."

"My point exactly. Food like that, amazing, mouth-watering, eye-rollingly good cuisine, has to come from here." He taps his breastbone. "It has to come from passion. From the artist inside the chef."

A grin spreads on my face. His enthusiasm is infectious, and my resistance to his charm is futile. I might as well wave the white flag now. "Have you never wanted to cook?"

"I'm terrible in the kitchen. But I love good food, and I crave the rush of investing, so this is the perfect combination for me. I get to be part of a business I love and participate in a way that fits my skills. Plus, I can spend more time with Hayden. Though this deal has taken more hours than I'd expected."

I lift a hand, meaning to rest it on his arm and reassure him. To tell him he's doing great, he's managing with just the right balance. But I stop, returning my hand to the table as I answer, "You know, I'm happy to help if you need me. I love hanging out with Hayden."

"You already do so much. And you're absolutely amazing with her. You must have been incredible with all your brothers."

"They were my little pack. I was their alpha dog," I joke, though it's true. "I'm the oldest of four, and the only girl, so helping raise kids comes naturally to me. Even though I was the Chihuahua-size leader of a pack of German Shepherds."

Simon narrows his eyes as if he's appraising me. He makes a so-so gesture. "Give yourself credit. I'd say you're more of a"—he taps his chin—"a *Fox* Terrier."

Holy shit. Did he just put the emphasis on *fox*?

I blush and try to think of something clever to say when the waiter arrives.

I offer to pay, but Simon shakes his head and peels off a few crisp bills. "You all set?"

I nod as I stand, shouldering my bag.

Looking at the remains of our meal, a wave of disappointment smacks me. The time with him is over. We had our tutoring, we had our chat, and now we will go our separate ways. I've had such a good time with him, and I don't want it to end. I want the afternoon to keep unfurling.

We step away from the café, and I find myself wondering what he'll do during the rest of the day, where he goes when he's not with his daughter. He'll probably work, but what if he doesn't? What if he's met someone? A lovely single mother who has a little girl, too? The thought horrifies me, and already I want to tackle that unknown woman and tell her to stay the hell away from him.

As we walk toward the subway station, Simon clears his throat. "There's a theater in Tribeca. It's showing nature documentaries as part of a film festival." His voice is dry, with a hint of nerves. He lifts his wrist and checks the time. "There's a film on zebras."

Then he blinks and shakes his head as if he just heard himself. "Wow. Did that ever sound weird?" His words keep tumbling from his lips as if he's never asked anyone to the movies before.

His awkwardness warms my heart and makes me beam. He's not seeing another woman. He wants to spend more time with me.

"But would you like to go see a film about zebras? I have a free afternoon—"

Before he can say another word, I clasp my hand on his arm and say yes. He wants what I want. "I would love to see a film about zebras."

CHAPTER TEN

Simon

When the young zebra is separated from his family, she gasps and clutches my arm.

When he evades a lion, she digs her nails into my bicep.

And when he's reunited with his striped friends and family, she clasps her hand over her mouth and turns to me. "Oh my God," she whispers through her fingers.

I calculate how big a check I should send to the Zebra Foundation because this hour-long documentary has turned out to be some kind of foreplay.

It's better than taking a woman to a horror flick in the hopes that she jumps into your arms. Not that I like horror films, and not that I've done that. But I had no clue the zebra's tale of survival would elicit this sort of reaction from Abby, who seems to *feel* every moment of what's happening onscreen deep in her bones.

I just wanted to do something nice for her, since she took the time out of her day to help me. But honestly, that's not entirely true. I didn't want to say goodbye to her. Little did I know a nature documentary would lead to her busy little hands squeezing my arm in a dark theater.

As the credits roll, she says, "My heart is still beating a hundred miles an hour."

"That's faster than a zebra at top speed."

She smiles and takes a steadying breath. "That was so good. Thank you for taking me," she says, and pride suffuses me. I love that she had the best time at this unexpected afternoon outing.

"My pleasure," I say, then my eyes stray to her hand, still wrapped around my arm. Some of the other moviegoers shuffle up the aisle, heading out of the darkened theater.

"Oh God, I'm sorry," she says and yanks her hand away.

"I really didn't mind," I say softly. "Glad my arm could be of service."

"I don't think I was even aware that I was gripping it like a lifeline during the film."

I was completely aware, and truth be told, it was my favorite part of the movie.

"I was just so into it," she says with a shrug. "I guess now you know why I like the eagles so much."

"I do. But I understood it before, too."

She tilts her head to ask, "Yeah?"

I nod. "You kind of light up when you watch them. Just like how you do when you talk about the Museum of Natural History. There's a sparkle in your eyes," I say, gesturing to those gorgeous amber-flecked eyes.

Her lips part. "I do?"

"You do, Abby. It's an innate part of you. Separate from languages, separate from your talent with kids. It's part of what makes you tick." Even as I say it, I worry this is where we're in real danger—talking about who we are, what we love, what makes us happy.

Maybe this is even riskier than my hands in her hair, or secret touches that hint of more. More dangerous than naughty little comments on skinny-dipping and lubricant. Perhaps this is the real fire—how I feel sitting here with her, our knees nearly touching, our elbows aligned, our gazes locked.

Everyone else leaves, and we don't move.

She licks her lips, swallows, and casts her eyes down. When she raises her face, she speaks softly. "You're right," she says, and her voice sounds vulnerable.

But inviting. Like she wants to talk, to get to know each other even more.

I tilt my head, curious. "Why do you like shows about wild animals so much?"

She seems to consider my question for a moment, then she answers, "For the same reason I like working with kids. It's real. No falseness. No pretense. That, and I've always been at home with wild dogs. Three brothers and all," she adds with a curve of her lips.

I return her smile with one of my own. "I like that. No, I love that. And that's what I loved, too, when you first showed me the Eagle Cam, and what I enjoyed about this film. They were never my thing before. Weren't even on my radar. But because of you I pay more attention, and when I do it's fascinating to watch what's truly real."

She nods enthusiastically. "Did you know eagles can sleep with one eye open?"

"Like a mobster?"

"Exactly! They're unihemispheric, I learned. They can sleep and be awake at the same time," she says, her eyes sparkling as she explains. "They truly do keep one eye open, and the awake part of the brain watches for predators. Dolphins are the same."

I wink slowly, showing her one closed eye.

She wags a finger at me. "But you didn't put half your brain to sleep."

"No, but I'm working on my unihemispheric potential."

She laughs, then says, "See? The natural world has so many wonders, and they're all real and true."

Real and true. I love the sound of those words. Especially because pretense was all I knew from Miriam during the last few years of our marriage, and especially the final months when she conducted her affair with a coworker. When her transgressions came to light, I was hurt. No surprise there. No one wants to be cheated on. But I wasn't as devastated as I thought I'd be. I met her shortly after college, but we'd been drifting apart for a long time. Honestly, I'd already pulled away from her emotionally, burying myself in work rather than dealing with the reality that we weren't right for each other anymore.

Maybe that was what had made it so easy to say what I did when I saw the text messages between her and the guy she worked with.

"Sleeping with your coworker, Miriam? That's a bit cliché."

"Working so hard you ignore your wife? That's a bit cliché," she'd fired back.

Neither one of us fought for the marriage. She was ready to leave. I was ready to let go of her. Now, a few years later, I don't pine for her at all. I'm just glad she's no longer my wife. I don't want her brand of pretense in a relationship.

I want this honesty, this openness—this *realness.*

That's what makes my longing for Abby so much tougher to manage. It's rooted in who she is. She's not fake. She's not phony. She's so fucking real and that makes me fall harder for her, and I wonder if she can tell. Seeing as I knew the show times for a zebra documentary, I'm not sure how it could be any more obvious that I've got it bad for her.

But I've played hooky for long enough. I need to catch up on work so I can devote my attention to Hayden come Monday morning when I have her for the week, as I usually do. She's with me most of the time, but we try to stay flexible, and Miriam plans to bring our daughter back early so she can jet to the nation's capital for business. She's a lobbyist, and her job suits her since she loves to make people's lives miserable.

The lights flicker on in the theater. An usher enters to pick up popcorn buckets and candy boxes.

Abby stands, smooths a hand over her yellow sundress, and grabs her purse. "Thank you for taking me to the movies," she says sweetly, but I swear the only words I truly hear are *taking me.*

God, how I want to take her. I want to take her to dinner, and I want to take her to my bed.

She walks up the aisle, and for those few seconds, I don't fight my lust. I check her out the entire way. Her legs are smooth and toned, but not too muscular. I bet they'd feel spectacular wrapped around me. Her hair glides down her back, and I want to rope my hands through it when I'm not practicing a braid. And then, there's her ass. I think—no, I'm sure that I could worship it. Plant kisses all over it, then spin her around, cup my hands on those luscious cheeks, and yank her close to me.

Fuck, now my dick is imitating an iron spike, and I might as well get a megaphone and announce that I've got a very big thing for her. In case that wasn't self-evident. When we reach the lobby, I find myself wishing I'd bought Junior Mints, just so I had a box of candy to cover up the salute in my jeans. And I don't even like mints.

Out on the busy street, Abby doesn't notice. Or maybe she just doesn't say anything. I hail a cab quickly, and we head uptown.

"We can drop you off first," I say, since she lives on the west side, and I'm on the east. That means the ride is up for her, and then all the way across town too, for me. New Yorkers never do this. We hate going up and over, but I'll gladly take the inconvenience for another few minutes with her. Then, it hits me. "Wait. I didn't even ask if you were heading home."

"I am. But then I'm going out," she says as the cab stops abruptly at a light. The radio plays faintly from the front seat, and the divider is mostly closed.

"Ah, well. Have fun," I say in my best chipper tone, and in this moment I couldn't be more aware of the barriers between us. She's going out because she has complete control of her own free time. I'm heading to work on a Friday evening so that my weekday mornings will be free to spend with my kid.

I wouldn't change a damn thing. My daughter is the love of my life. But I'm also keenly aware that this simple fact makes me the wrong choice for Abby. My time is limited. My attention is already spoken for.

"I will have fun," Abby says. "I'm seeing Harper and Nick, and Spencer and Charlotte. We're all going to play pool, even though I'm terrible."

My ears prick. "I'm awesome at pool," I say, because it's true and I can't resist dropping in this tidbit. Maybe I want to impress her. Hell, I definitely want to impress her.

Her eyebrows rise. "You are?"

"Paid for a few classes in college as a pool shark."

Her jaw drops. "No! You never told me that!"

I shrug casually as the driver speeds up, trying to race through a light. He veers into the next lane in an attempt to stay ahead of the traffic. "Don't I seem like a pool hustler?"

She narrows her eyes and grips her purse strap, as if that will help her hold on as this guy drives more dangerously than he should. "No. Not at all."

"I played at night and won some money in a few games," I say with a big grin as the cab swerves again and we cross into Chelsea. The car cuts so quickly, Abby jams her hand against the divider to hold on.

"You okay?" I ask her.

She nods and lowers her voice. "He's a little aggressive behind the wheel."

I clear my throat and lean forward to talk to the driver through the small window. "Hey, man. We're not in a rush, so let's just be a little more steady as she goes."

The driver grumbles something that sounds like *yes*, and I lean back against the black leather seat.

"Thank you," she says, with a small curve in her lips. "You're my hero."

Oh hell. Those words. Her lips. The look in her eyes. I blurt out the next thing that comes to mind. "I can help you play."

"You can?"

The cab veers into another lane, sending Abby shooting closer to me. Suddenly, she's inches away, her face close to mine, her hand on my shoulder. I don't know how this has happened, but we've gone once again from a simple conversation to the cusp of more.

I lick my lips once, my gaze drifting briefly to her hand. "I'll teach you sometime. I'm a good pool tutor."

She nods and curls her fingers tighter. "I bet you are."

"I thought you didn't believe me?"

"I do," she says softly, her eyes vulnerable and honest. "I do believe you."

And I don't care about the driver right now, or whether he's going to Frogger it up the rest of the avenue. I definitely don't give a shit about how little time and attention I have to spare. I barely care about anything but what my heart and body want right now.

This woman, who won't let go of her hold on me.

"Believe me," I whisper, then raise my hand and gently finger the strands of her hair.

She leans closer, and I move to her, and then she grips the collar of my shirt.

"*Simon*," she whispers. Her voice sounds beautifully desperate—like how I feel with her.

There are no more decisions to be made.

I inch closer, our faces nearly touching. I can feel her breath on me. Our noses brush, then I slant my mouth to hers. Our lips touch, and it's like a world that was ordinary has now turned extraordinary.

I cup her cheeks, holding her face as I deepen the kiss. More lips, more tongue, more teeth. More Abby.

My entire body is alive. My heart pounds, my brain fires, and I'm wildly turned on. I've gone to bed many nights drifting off to the fantasy of this kind of hungry, frenzied, unexpected kiss. In my dirty dreams, the kisses turn into much more, and I touch her, taste her . . .

Take her.

But hell, a kiss is more than enough because this feels like the way kissing was meant to be—her hand clutching my shoulder, mine on her face, our lips caressing. Heat pulses through me, and at last, at long fucking last, the woman I've longed for wants me exactly the same way.

The yellow cab shimmies along the asphalt, and I'm lost in a kiss I barely saw coming, one I'm powerless to stop.

CHAPTER ELEVEN

Abby

This man can kiss. His lips taste so good as he kisses me with a tenderness and a hunger that's entirely new in my experience.

This kiss vibrates and spreads through my entire body, as if I've been shot full of liquid beauty, like gold and silver flow through my veins. He slides his tongue across mine, and I want to grab him, straddle him, and just kiss the daylights out of him, even in this crazy, dangerous cab.

I hardly care that our first kiss isn't on a moonlit balcony or under the stars. This kiss was inevitable, especially after the last few nights, all these days, and then this afternoon. All our moments have been marching to this as Simon kisses me with such reverence that I want to melt into him. I rope my fingers through his soft hair, and I truly can't believe I'm making out with Simon Travers in the back of a cab after we watched a documentary on zebras.

I wish I could say that alarms sound, telling me how risky it is to kiss the man I work for. But all I hear is the rapid beat of my heart, leading me closer to him.

Simon runs his thumb along my cheek, and that soft touch makes me tremble. Somehow I wriggle closer, my breasts pressed to his firm chest. He groans. It's carnal and masculine, almost like a warning. But neither one of us heeds it. We simply can't stop. We're *those* people. The kind who go crazy in public. I feel insane right now. Crazy and wild and reckless.

His hands are on my face, then my hair, and then the back of my head. He is all heat and passion. The way his lips sweep over mine, the way his tongue explores my mouth, and most of all, the way he holds me—it all makes me want to grab those strong shoulders of his and slam him down on top of my body. I want to feel him slide my wrists over my head, pin them, and then smother me in kisses everywhere. I want to let go beneath his mouth, arch into him, urge him to explore my body the way he seems to want to.

The car jerks to a stop.

Abruptly, we separate, but only slightly.

He blinks and breathes out hard as he glances around. We're all the way in Columbus Circle. Holy shit. We kissed for blocks upon blocks.

My lips miss his. I thread my hand into his hair. "We shouldn't do this," I say, though it hardly sounds like a protest as his hair falls through my fingers.

His eyes float closed, and his mouth is open, his breath coming in harsh pants. "We definitely shouldn't do this," he says, his voice low and smoky as he sighs deeply at my touch.

"You're my boss," I say, pointing out the obvious.

"You're my—"

Whatever he was going to say next is cut off when he brushes his lips against my forehead, then over my face, dusting my cheek, my eyelids, my jawline.

My skin sizzles. My stomach flips. I want to live inside this kiss. "Don't stop," I murmur as his lips mark me.

He travels to my neck, and I tilt my head to the side. He layers kisses all along the column of my throat, the delicious mix of his rough stubble and his soft lips sending sparks to my very core. My body is hungry, eager for him, and I'm going to need a new word for *want* because what I feel for Simon is so much more than that.

It's yearning. It's non-negotiable. I have to have him.

"I don't know that I can stop with you, Abby," he whispers, and my name falling from his lips is exquisite and sensual.

In it, I hear his complete and utter need for me, and it's thrilling—because it matches my heart. It matches my body, too.

His lips return to me, and we give in once more to the desire that's thrummed between us for months. I used to think these feelings were all in my mind. Then, in the last few days, I knew they were returned. Funny how once we left the confines of his house, it only took a couple of hours for tutoring to turn into wine, food, and conversation, then to grabbing him in the dark theater.

My God, what was I thinking, putting my hands all over him during the movie?

This.

I was thinking I wanted *this.*

His stubbled jaw brushes against my face, and I love the feel of it, the whiskery burn it'll leave on my skin. My hands roam along his arms, traveling to his biceps, so firm and strong, and immediately I'm awash in images and possibilities. Sliding under him. Those strong arms anchored above me. Running my hands along his muscles as he moves in me. The images blaze hard and hot.

A wave of neon heat rolls through me, lighting me up all over, settling between my legs where I truly do ache for him. This man isn't just turning me on. He's turning me into a woman who wants only to be taken.

He kisses deeper, harder, rougher—like he needs me desperately. God, I need this kiss, too. I'm so far gone, and I'm sure he is too, judging from the groans he makes as he devours my lips. His hands travel all over my body, exploring my waist, my shoulders, and my neck. His hands dive into my hair, his fingers threading tightly. It feels incredible. He clasps my head possessively, and I'm a blur of sparks and sensation.

This is more than touching—more than kissing. It's like a claiming, the way his lips consume mine, how his hands

THE SEXY ONE · 99

grip my head. I can't get enough of him, and he can't get enough of me, either. That realization crashes into me beautifully. Seductively. Flooding me with so much heat.

I grab at him, taking all he has to give, letting him kiss me like the world hangs in the balance.

Then, my skull bonks the headrest.

"Ow," I mutter, as the cab swings onto a side street and we separate. This driver is a big buzzkill.

"Cabs," I mumble as I catch my breath. When I meet Simon's gaze, his blue eyes shine with desire. "Hard to make out in cabs."

"But I'm willing to keep trying," he says, with a quirk of his lips.

"How magnanimous of you."

He smiles, then threads his hand through my hair once more and presses his lips to my forehead. It's soft and intimate, and it makes me long for more of him. Then, because my desire for him momentarily displaces all sanity, I raise my face and ask, "Do you want to go out with us tonight?"

He cringes as if I've said the lamest thing.

Crap. I just asked him on a date. I'm a world-class idiot. "I'm sorry. I just thought because of pool and all. You said you'd teach me. But I'm sure you're busy."

He parts his lips to speak, but he's silent as the car slows at the curb. Dragging a hand through his hair, he heaves a sigh. "Thank you. But I don't think that's a good idea."

My heart falls with a heavy thud, and I back away from him.

"Right," I say, nearly choking on the word. I wave a hand in the air, as if I can erase the stupid, impulsive moment when I asked out the father of the girl I nanny for. There's no way he wants to hang out with my friends and me. He has a real life, and real responsibilities. He's only kissing me like his life depends on it because of pent-up lust, not from a desire to spend an evening with the gang.

"Abby," he says, and his tone touches on desperation, but whatever is coming next is cut off by the driver who taps the glass and announces the amount.

"I'll take care of it. I'm heading across town," Simon says to the driver as I sling my purse onto my shoulder.

He looks at me. "About tonight. It's just—"

He stops, blinks, and points to the window.

I follow his gaze. My friends wait for me on the stoop to my apartment. Harper and her fiancé, Nick, lean against the stone wall, his arms wrapped around her as she laughs at something he says. I didn't think we were meeting up for an hour, but I might have gotten the time wrong.

"Your friends are here." Simon's voice is strained.

Harper untangles herself from Nick and waves at me. My eyes swing back to Simon, and he looks guilty, even though no one saw us kissing. But just as quickly, his expression shifts to friendly as he gives a brief wave to Harper and Nick.

"I should go."

"Abby," he says again, as if it's the start of a plea.

But I don't know what either one of us is supposed to say about what just happened. Instead, I guide us to safer ground. "I'll see you . . . on Monday." I lift my chin, reminding myself that I have a job to do. Whatever else those last fifteen magnificent minutes were, they were temporary. A blip. "We'll just focus on work. Right?"

He nods slowly, as if he's processing this new plan. "Work," he says, like he's never heard the word. Then his voice turns crisp and resolute. "Yes, work."

"Pretend it never happened," I add, because the more I say it, the more we can move on and erase this mistake.

"Is that what you want?" he asks, like it costs him something.

No. I want to kiss you all over again, all night long. I want you to take me upstairs, strip me naked, and make love to me the way you kissed me. With everything you have. With your heart, body and soul.

"I just think . . ." My voice falters. I'm not ready to have this conversation, not when my deepest wishes are caught in my throat. "I better go."

"I understand. Good night, Abby," he says, and he sounds pained. "Have fun."

"I will," I say, doing my best impression of a cheery, happy gal.

I slide out of the car and leave the best kiss of my life behind.

When Harper saunters over, she arches an eyebrow. "Boss dropping you off now?"

"I'm tutoring him in French," I say, as the sound of the cab squealing away from the curb rips through the air. I refocus, rooting myself to this moment, to my real life, which has nothing to do with making out with the father of the girl I take care of. The kiss was a one-time thing, and now I need to slide back into who I am. "Why are you here already?"

Harper flashes an easy grin. "We were in the neighborhood and decided to see if you wanted to start happy hour early. It is Friday after all."

I grit my teeth, draw a quick inhale, and do a reboot of the day. "Let's do it," I say with a crisp nod. "I need a big, fat glass of wine."

Harper laughs and threads her arm through mine. "Wine it is. Get your ID out, sweet little thing."

She links her other arm with Nick's, and the three of us head to our favorite bar for happy hour, where I focus on them, not my forbidden fantasy with Simon.

This is my real life, with my friends. They are my family here in New York.

CHAPTER TWELVE

Simon

Pretend it never happened.
   Pretend it never happened.
   Pretend it never happened.

Her words play in my head all weekend long. As I review pitches and proposals from business associates, as I respond to an email from Gabriel, as I work out at the gym, and as I meet my older sister, Kristy, for lunch on Saturday in Gramercy Park, where she lives.

As I listen to my sister tell me the latest about her fashion design business, I pretend I never kissed Abby. Over appetizers, Kristy updates me on the new distribution deals she's inked for her upcoming lines, and I try to fight away the lingering memory of Abby's lips. My sister asks me something about a partnership, as I drift back to how that woman responded to me as if our kiss was as necessary as food and water. As if it was inevitable.

We'd smashed together as if we unlocked the other's desire. Then, she'd simply melted in my arms. Fuck, I'm dying for another taste of Abby.

Frustrated doesn't even begin to cover how I feel right now. As I drag a hand over the back of my neck, Kristy delivers a steely stare. "You're distracted, Simon," she says with that hawk-eyed awareness that all older sisters possess.

Busted.

"Just a lot going on," I admit. "But tell me again about the partnership."

Kristy arches an eyebrow as she picks up her mint tea. We're trying out a Turkish restaurant today. "Don't worry about me. Is it Miriam? Is she being a total twat about custody of Hayden?"

I give her a look. "Can you not use the word twat in the same sentence as my daughter?"

She rolls her green eyes. "You're so prickly. I was talking about your ex, not your sweet girl."

I ease up. "I know. Sorry. She's just being Miriam, but you know she's a good mother. She's good to Hayden on the weekends she has her, and she's fine with the arrangement." I aim to practice civility post-divorce. It's far too easy to hate an ex, but it's a pointless expenditure of emotion, and one I don't care to spend on Miriam. She only gave me a hard time in the beginning, but then she easily agreed to me having primary custody.

"It's a damn good thing that woman adores *my* precious niece," Kristy says, with her own fierce protectiveness of

Hayden. Then she raises her fists. "Or I'd have to go *Fight Club* on the former Mrs. Travers."

I laugh. "No need to take off the gloves."

My sister runs a hand through her dark brown hair, narrows her eyes, and then nods reluctantly. "Fair enough." She lowers her voice to a whisper, "But I'm probably always going to think Miriam is a twat."

I manage a small smile. "You're well within your rights."

"And business is good?"

"Very good," I say, then catch her up to speed on the latest from Gabriel. "He has the pick of investors, though, so I've got to convince him to go with me. I've been doing my research, and it's taking a lot of time. Especially since he wants to do more than open a restaurant here. He has plans for a whole slate of them, a cookware line, recipe books—the whole shebang."

"Sounds like a lot of work." She reaches her hand across the table and places her palm on my arm. "Are you burning the candle at both ends again?"

Like I said, Kristy was created with 100 hundred percent big-sister ingredients.

"I'm fine," I say, taking a drink of my water as I gesture for the check.

"*Fine*? You said you were fine when you were working on Wall Street, too. But you weren't. You were working too much. It was killing you."

I drag a hand through my hair. "And I left when Hayden was young, so it's all good. I get to spend a lot of time with her now that I've rearranged my schedule and workload," I say, though she may have a point.

Finding the right balance has always been my biggest challenge. It's still one, because work has been my steady companion since my marriage cratered. The new job in restaurant investing helped me through the divorce. It gave me a focus. It was reliable, regular, and it didn't screw someone else behind my back. But lately, this new restaurant deal has started to consume more of me.

"Okay," my sister says, but her tone makes it clear she doesn't believe me. "Suppose this is all true. Why are you so out of sorts today? Is it just work, sweetie?" She takes a drink of her tea then sets it down on the table. "Or something else?"

I shake my head, bemused. "You're too astute."

She smirks. "I am. It's vexing to you, isn't it? My uncanny ability to read you?"

"Vexing is precisely what *you* are." I shift gears, answering her, but admitting nothing. "And yes, I've got something on my mind. But it won't be on my mind much longer. I promise. Okay?"

She raises one eyebrow. "Do you want to talk about it?"

I shake my head. "I don't. But it's nothing to worry about."

"I can't *not* worry about my baby brother."

For a moment, I wonder if Abby feels the same about her three brothers. If she worries about their hearts, their lives, their choices.

The waiter arrives with the bill, and I'm thankful for the distraction. I don't want to tread on why I'm out of sorts, because it's stupid and pointless, and I wish I hadn't felt like such a dirty old man when we'd pulled up to Abby's home yesterday.

Seeing her friends waiting for her was a smack of reality. She has a whole life that's entirely different from mine, and that's not just because of the years between us. On the one hand, an eight-year age difference is hardly anything in the grand scheme of things. On the other, this isn't about the years that separate us. It's about the *situation*. I was so damn tempted to say yes to her offer to hang out and play pool on Friday night, but had we gone out together, it would have been painfully clear that I was the odd man out. The single dad. The divorced dude. The employer crushing on the nanny. The one-of-these-things-just-doesn't-belong.

Sure, Abby likes working with children, and she's great with them. But there's a difference between working with kids and being responsible for one.

I don't want to drag Abby down with all my baggage when her future is bright and amazingly free of luggage, except the kind she'd take on a trip to Prague, or Vienna, or Tokyo. I can picture her perfectly with her adventure-some spirit, exploring all those cities. That's what she should be free to do. I want her to have that unencumbered life.

I tuck my credit card into my wallet, say goodbye to my sister, and head to my office. Once there, though, I'm pretty sure I set a new record for my own distraction. Because . . . That. Fucking. Kiss.

Her taste. Her sweet breath. The scent of her skin. I've dreamed of it. Now I've had it, and it's better than all those dirty moments in my head. Her scent like coconut. Her breasts crushed against my chest. The way her hands explored my hair, my shoulders, my arms. The sexy little murmurs she made.

I whimper.

I'm ashamed that I'm a grown man whimpering.

I drop my forehead to my desk and bang it lightly a few times. I don't know why I even thought I could pretend it never happened. Tell that lie to the heart. Tell that fable to my dick. The rebellious bastard doesn't like the fact that Abby is off-limits. I'm fucking aroused at my desk on a Saturday evening, and the temptation is strong to take care of this persistent wood right now.

But even though I want to scoop up Abby into my arms, carry her to my bedroom, and strip off all her clothes so I can fuck her and make love to her at the same

THE SEXY ONE · 109

damn time, I can't go down this path. I might have stepped over a line yesterday, but that doesn't give me permission to do it again. That's the thing about lines. We make them, we break them, and we keep them.

This is a line I need to maintain.

My precious, sweet Hayden is the reason I need to behave.

I looked long and hard for a nanny so I could balance work and parenting. Last fall, I scoured the top Manhattan agencies, searched online, and asked for recommendations from other parents. Honestly, it wasn't until I thought to ask Harper for coffee and advice when she was helping me plan Hayden's birthday party that I was able to find the person I wanted for my girl. Harper made the perfect match. Abby's amazing with my daughter, and Hayden adores her. She's not a mom replacement and has never tried to be. She's simply fantastic at her job as a caretaker. I need her in my life in that role, not as a lover.

Which means . . .

Dick, stand down.

Brain, you're at bat.

I don't give into temptation that night. Not when I'm home alone, my mind tripping back to the cab, my body wanting her, my hand ready to take on its reliable job of steering a solo flight. Hell, getting off while imagining her has become a habit. Maybe that makes me a horny guy. But if the shoe fits . . .

Tonight, though, I'm going to be good.

I grab the remote and flick the channel to some military battle show. Ah, men in wool is a grade-A, top-choice turn-off, and this D-Day reenactment does the deflation trick quite nicely.

The rest of the evening is smooth sailing. I practice some of the French phrases I need for business. I text my buddy Tyler about our meet-up tomorrow morning. And I catch up on the latest business news.

There. Piece of cake. Getting Abby out of my system is easy.

But the next day when I check out the Eagle Cam and see the baby birds testing their wings, my resistance flies the coop. My heart skips a beat, knowing she'll love this. I can't *not* share this with her. I snap a screengrab and text it to Abby.

Simon: They'll be doing flight practice in no time . . . and before we know it, they'll be sleeping with one eye open.

She responds with a simple note.

Abby: Cute! Still on for French on Monday? I thought I could work with you while Hayden does the jungle coloring book I'm bringing her.

My heart craters.

And that, folks, is the other reason why I need to put on blinders.

She already has.

CHAPTER THIRTEEN

Simon

The basketball sails through the air, bouncing on the rim and spinning, then it drops through the net. I raise my arms victoriously.

"And that's another one in the can for this guy." I point my thumbs at myself, only because it drives Tyler crazy.

My friend shakes his head begrudgingly. "Lucky bastard," he says as he grabs the ball on the rebound and dribbles.

I raise my eyebrows and smirk. "It's not luck if I can do it again." I've already landed two in a row in our three-point session after our one-on-one.

It's seven on Sunday morning at the basketball court in Central Park where we shoot hoops once or twice a week.

Bouncing back and forth on the balls of his feet, Tyler raises his chin. "I've got a hundred dollars that says you can't do it a third time."

"I love your bets. It's like . . . wait." I pause, stroking my chin as he narrows his dark eyes at me. I hold up a finger. "I've got it. I know what it's like."

"What is it like?" he asks, exaggerated annoyance in his tone.

I mime tugging something off a branch. "It's like plucking money off a tree."

He tosses his head back and laughs. "You wish. There's no fucking way you're sinking another three-pointer. Le-Bron James you are not."

I scoff. "But I don't need to be the king." I return to the three-point line, and Tyler spreads his feet and gets in my face as he tries to defend. But I outmaneuver him, thanks to longer arms and natural skills at the game. When I release the ball, it arcs through the air and swooshes into the net. "All I have to do is get it past *you*."

"Fuck me," Tyler says, watching the ball bounce on the concrete as he drags a hand through his dark brown hair.

Tyler's a couple of years younger than me, and works in entertainment law. The man is known for his daring approach to deals, and his willingness to chase risks for his clients. Trouble is, he should know by now that betting against me on the court is a mistake. Basketball is just something that comes easily to me. Like languages do for—

"What do you say we go double or nothing on the Yankees going all the way this year?" I'm not a big gambler, but I've got to keep my mind on anything but that woman.

He mimes stabbing his chest. "Hit me in the heart, why don't you? You know I'm a Dodgers man. I would never take a bet on that New York team winning everything. Or anything," he says with a derision he reserves only for the boys in pinstripes.

I rub my thumb and forefinger together. "Then hand over a crisp Benjamin Franklin. Feel free to add a side of humble pie and then some crow for you to eat, too."

"You're such a fucker, Travers. You'll probably use it at a strip club." He grabs the ball and tucks it under his arm as we walk off the court.

I laugh and shake my head. "Now, you know there's a one hundred percent chance of that not happening, right?"

He claps me on the back. "That I *know* is a safe bet."

"There's this thing that happens when you have a daughter. You can pretty much never set foot in a strip club again. Unless it's to take a long trench coat inside and, I don't know, rescue a friend's kid or something," I say with a shrug. Fact is, I was never into that scene before my marriage, and it's certainly not something I'm eager to partake of now. I've been invited to a few for bachelor parties lately. I've declined the strip club portion of the boys' nights out.

"I hear ya on that one. I guess you can just put it in your piggybank then," he says, taking out his wallet and rifling through it for a bill. He hands me one.

I take it and hold it up. "You want it back?"

He laughs. "Course I do."

I fold it and stuff it inside my boxer briefs underneath my gym shorts. "Want it now?"

He cringes. "If you gave it to me I would burn it."

I laugh. "Excellent. I know exactly which bill I'll be using to buy drinks next time I see your sorry ass," I tell him, since we never use our winnings for anything but drinks or dinner the next time we connect.

As we near the path at the edge of Central Park, Tyler clears his throat. "So what's the latest? You met anyone?"

I shoot him a look as if he's crazy. "It's not as if I've been looking."

"But you're not *not* looking?"

"Such a lawyer," I say, laughing. "Always turning language around."

He holds up his hands in surrender. "All I did was make a double negative. But do feel free to answer the question, unless you want a ruthless cross-examination. Have you met anyone during your not *not* looking?"

We weave past early morning joggers and cyclists on the loop. As we near Fifth Avenue, I take a breath and decide what the hell? If I told my sister, she'd want to comfort me, advise me, and guide me through the Abby situation. But Bungee Jump Tyler, as his cousin calls him? Considering the guy's got his sights set on winning back the woman he was once crazy for, and he stands such a minute chance of succeeding, it's a sure bet he'll *get* my impossible romantic situation.

"There is someone. But I can't have her. Tell me, what do you do when you want someone you can't have?"

He nods sagely and taps his temple. "I got your answer right here."

"Knew I could count on you. Tell me your secret."

He holds up his right hand and makes the international symbol for self-love. "You spend a lot of nights reading your fortune."

I roll my eyes. "Seriously? That's your trick?"

He peers at his hand and pretends to study it. "My lifeline is going to be nice and long, on account of regular use of the hand brake." As a bus rumbles along the avenue, he adopts a more serious tone. "Who is she? This *untouchable*?"

I stop at the crosswalk and turn to face him. No point hemming and hawing. "The nanny."

His jaw drops. His eyes widen. And he blows out a long stream of air. "Didn't see that coming. Damn. You and Ben Affleck."

I protest indignantly. "No. Not at all like Ben Affleck. Seeing as he cheated on his wife."

"True that." Tyler snaps his fingers. "*The Sound of Music*. The father and the nanny. Well, technically she was the governess."

"And didn't he have eight kids or something? Are you just trying to kill me now?"

"One. Eight. What's the difference?"

"Sanity, man. Sanity is the difference. Besides, since when do you know the storyline of *The Sound of Music* so well?"

"I represent the director of the Broadway revival, asshole," Tyler says, laughing at me. "Besides, even if I didn't, there's nothing wrong with being culturally literate."

"Never said there was."

"Are you two . . .?" he asks as we cross the street.

I shake my head, answering his unfinished question. "We had a brief . . . moment." Though that hardly does the cab ride justice. That was the culmination of a million moments.

"Impressive. Didn't think you had it in you, Simon."

"Nor did I."

"But you're going to stay the fuck away from that?"

"Yeah, I think so." I take a deep breath. "But is what I've done so far really that bad?" I ask, and this time there's no trash talking, no giving each other a hard time. I ask him frankly, needing his honest appraisal. At his core, Tyler is an upfront kind of friend.

"You're fine. Considering you're not in Affleck's situation, it's not that bad. If you want to keep her as your employee, then it wouldn't be your wisest choice to have any more . . . moments." He slows his pace as we reach the block where I live. "But you knew that."

I nod. "I do know that."

* * *

When Miriam arrives on Monday morning, she issues a curt hello. She's suited up, her dark hair slicked into a bun, ready for business. Then, as if she just remembered our post-split vow to not be assholes, she flashes a smile. "How was your weekend?"

What a loaded fucking question. Only she has no idea, so I keep the answer simple. "Great. I got a lot of work done. Did you two have fun together?"

Hayden gazes up at her mother and answers for both of them. "Yes! We always do. And there's something I have to find right now, but it's a secret." She takes off for her room like a tornado.

Miriam fiddles with her purse clasp, clearly ready to go. "I'll be back in a week. I'm meeting with lawmakers up-state, and we have a lot of ground to cover, but I should be home in time to have her Saturday night."

"Sounds like a plan."

"See you then. Have a good week." She turns to leave, then pauses. "Oh. She sneezed a few times this weekend." She gestures to the couch and living room. "You might want to get your maid here more often. All this dust will only make Hayden's allergies worse."

I rub a hand across the back of my neck. For starters, my home isn't dirty. But that's beside the point. "Hayden does not have allergies."

Miriam raises her chin. "Well, she could." She taps her chest. "I have allergies."

"Then it's a good thing you don't live here," I say, plastering on a tight grin.

"You don't have to be like that."

"If you feel the need to criticize my *clean* home, then I do need to be like that." I heave a sigh. "Please. Let's just be civil."

"I was civil. I said to have a good week."

"Civil also means no unnecessary insults about my home."

She huffs, then nods. "Fine. I was simply worried about her. Allergies are no fun, and I don't want her to have any."

"And I will continue to be on a full allergy alert," I say, even though Hayden's never once shown a sign of them.

"Thank you. Have a good week," she says, and then leaves.

I shut the door behind her, the *click* of the lock a satisfying sound, separating her from me. I make my way to Hayden's room, where she's curled over her toy chest, searching it. A true smile spreads on my face as I watch her hunt. She's victorious when she finds a wooden sword, pops up, and challenges me to a duel. *"En garde!"*

Immediately, I grab the matching sword, adopt a *Three Musketeers* stance, and proceed to fence with my daughter for the next five minutes.

When she stabs me in the belly, I crumple to the ground and clutch at my wound.

"Oh no! We have to save you," she says, kneeling.

"Help, help," I call out, clasping my chest.

"Don't worry. I have a Band-Aid."

"Hurry, nurse. Please hurry."

She rushes to her toy chest, grabs a white plastic first-aid kit for kids, and procures a Hello Kitty Band-Aid. "It's my secret supply," she whispers, then opens the Band-Aid and presses it on my shirt.

I pop back up immediately and declare, "It's a miracle! I'm all better."

She wipes a hand on her brow. "I was so worried." She tilts her head. "Daddy, I think I want to take fencing lessons."

I arch an eyebrow as I lean against her bed. "Yeah? What inspired that?"

"I watched *Puss in Boots* this weekend at Mommy's."

"That sounds like an excellent reason to learn how to fence. Want me to look into it?" She nods excitedly as I look at my watch. "All right, sweet pea. It's nine in the morning. I go into the office at one. Want to do anything special before lunch?"

She sticks out a sandaled foot at me, showing me her nails. Cotton-candy pink polish has worn down to mere specks. "My nails look terrible. Can I get a pedicure?"

"Yes, but you know the rule."

"No red or black," she says.

"But go crazy with the pastels," I tell her.

She reaches for my offered hand, and like that, with her small fingers laced through my big ones, we head to her favorite salon around the block. They know her at Daisy Nails, and treat her like a princess, as well as the regular customer that she is.

Daisy, the owner, looks up from the brush, flashing me a crooked smile as a sheet of dark hair falls across her cheek. "You want one, too, Hayden's daddy?"

That's what she calls me, and that's fine with me. "Nah, I'm trying to cut back."

"Pedicures are good for you," she says playfully. Every time I'm here, she makes a valiant attempt to get me in the chair.

"That so? New medical study come out on the topic?"

"Lots of men get pedicures these days. It's important to have handsome feet," Daisy says, patting a big brown chair next to my girl.

"Yes, Daddy. Do it!" Hayden calls out from her perch. "You can have handsome feet!"

"Aren't my feet already good-looking?" I give an exaggerated wiggle of my toes inside my shoes.

"C'mon," Hayden shouts with a smile.

I shake my head. "I'm holding out on you both. No pedicure for me today."

"Next time then," Daisy says. "I won't stop till you're in the chair."

"I'll consider myself forewarned."

I spend the rest of the time making funny faces for Hayden and keeping her in stitches as she has her toes painted silver and purple. "Can I get a flower on the big toe?" she asks as Daisy finishes the color.

"Did you make your bed when you were at your mom's?"

"I did all my chores."

"And all last week with me?"

"I did."

"And did you listen to Abby when you were with her?"

"I always listen to Abby," she says, and the way she says her nanny's name squeezes my chest. Hayden says it with sweetness, with earnestness. She adores Abby, and Abby adores her.

I scrub a hand across my jaw, wishing I didn't love their connection so much. "Then you can get a flower."

After, I take her out to lunch at her favorite diner where we feast on chicken sandwiches and French fries, and the weight in my gut doesn't come from the food but from the knowledge that the real playacting starts in thirty minutes when Abby arrives for work.

We return home, and a few minutes later, Abby's here.

At the sound of the knock, I draw a deep breath and head to the door, my feet heavy, my nerves racing, and my dumb heart still pounding hard. I'm like a buffet of warring emotions—lust, desire, regret, and hope all tossed together, chopped and julienned.

But when I open the door, one single emotion fights its way to the front of the pack as my breath catches in my throat. Desire wins, and it comes from the body and from the mind. She's so gorgeous. Her wild blond hair is loose over her shoulders, and she sports an orange V-neck T-shirt, and a summery, flowered skirt. As usual, she hardly wears any makeup, and she looks good enough to kiss.

Obviously.

I'm right back where I shouldn't be—thinking of touching her. Of how utterly fucking spectacular it was to taste her lips. How she practically climbed on me. How she felt in my arms, so warm and perfect, wanting what I had to give her.

"Good to see you," I say, and my voice sounds like it comes from another planet.

She smiles brightly. Too brightly. "Good to see you, Mr. Travers."

I wince as she puts space between us by using my last name. "Simon. No one calls me Mr. Travers," I say gently. But maybe this distance, this formality, is what she needs to deal with my transgression.

She nods and then holds out her arms for Hayden, who crashes into them in a big hug. "What do you want to do today, crazy girl? Because I have some wild ideas."

"Oh tell me, tell me, tell me," Hayden says, bouncing up and down.

Abby doesn't look at me. She only has eyes for my daughter as she shares her plans for their day.

Unlike me, she doesn't seem to have any trouble pretending it never happened, and that's an invisible fist to the gut. The blow hurts more than I ever expected, even though I've seen it coming for days.

CHAPTER FOURTEEN

Abby

After we explore both the funky and the traditional nooks in Chinatown that afternoon, Hayden face-plants on her bed, snoozing in seconds. I press a kiss to her wild hair and cover her with a maroon paw-print throw blanket. Her regular comforter is in the laundry.

As I tug the soft material to her shoulders, I remember something Simon once said when I was hunting in the linen closet, and I'd asked him if he knew where the nap blanket was.

"Why does that term exist?"

"What term?"

"Nap blanket. I don't get it," he said, scratching his head. "It's smaller than a regular blanket. Does that mean you're smaller when you nap?"

I'd laughed. "Of course. Science has proven we become tinier during an afternoon snooze."

He'd beamed. "There you go."

As I leave Hayden's room, the memory brings a smile to my face. His observation had amused me then; it has the same effect now.

We've always had an easy rapport. Always gotten along. Sure, he's been my boss. He's been the man in charge, and the one who signs my paychecks, but it's never felt like a work relationship where power flows from the top of the hill to the lowly employees at the bottom.

We joke. We tease. We talk.

He's always felt like a . . . friend, even though I have a crush on him. But a friend nonetheless.

I want to make sure we can be that way again. Not just boss and employee, but friends . . . nap-blanket friends.

With the door shut, I tread quietly across the carpet, grab my phone from my bag, and set the alarm for forty-five minutes. If I let Hayden nap too long she'll never go to sleep at night, but she's tired since we covered a lot of ground sampling soft buns and noodles, hunting through quirky boutiques, and eating fortune cookies.

In a tchotchke shop full of embroidered jackets, fans, and other little items, she'd asked me so politely for one of those red and gold cats with the ceaselessly waving paw that I'd picked one up for her, then a back scratcher for her friend Madison on the third floor of the building, and then she'd wanted to bring a bamboo plant to her dad for good luck with his business deal.

As I'd plunked down the bills at the counter, my heart had twisted with a strange combination of guilt, shame, and, oddly, excitement at buying something for Simon, even if it was actually from his daughter. The most dangerous organ in my chest had been shouting at the little girl, *Your father is amazing and I'm crazy for him.*

Then my brain had scoffed and said, *Don't be a fool. Stop fantasizing about this girl's daddy.*

The man I'm crazy for is the father of this precious, sweet, adventuresome, wonderful girl. I want her in my life, and I need this job.

That ought to make him easy to resist.

Ought.

Scooting back into the pillows on the chocolate-brown couch in the living room, I click open my text messages to find one from Harper.

Harper: Soooo???? How was it? Did you manage seeing His Hotness?

I smile faintly. I'd told Harper everything Friday night about what happened in the cab, and how it had been like a dam bursting between us, then how it had slammed shut when he'd turned me down.

Abby: I survived. It was hard. I put on my game face when I arrived. But as you know, my game face sucks.

I insert an emoticon of a fox with his eyes narrowed, his lips a thin line. Then I add another text.

Abby: Dude, do I not have the best emoticons ever?

Harper: You so do. :) But do you think he could tell it was your game face?

I consider her question. Simon certainly seemed to be doing his best this morning to be cordial, and to follow my directive to pretend nothing had happened.

Abby: I guess I need to give him credit for doing what I asked. He was unruffled.

Harper: Is that what you want?

Abby: You know I barely have a clue what I want.

Harper: Not true. You do know. And you know what you need to do.

She means the advice she gave me when I'd pulled her into the ladies' room of the pool hall. "Tell me what to do," I'd said, gripping her arm, desperate for something, anything. "I'm so crazy about him, and it's so wrong, but I want it to be right."

She'd smiled sympathetically, brushing an errant strand of hair from my face. "The situation is complicated, and I can't tell you what to do. But at the very least, you should try to talk to him."

She's too damn smart. Talking to him about the longing I have for him gives me the willies. It's akin to lacing up sneakers and going for a run. I shudder at the mere prospect of both. And I'm a talker, so that should make it abundantly clear how terrified I am of voicing my feelings.

Abby: My mouth was superglued closed last night by little green men. Guess I won't be able to talk to His Hotness now.

Harper: Bummer. Guess you can't do anything else with that mouth, either. Like kiss him again. Or more.

Abby: You're evil.

Harper: But you love me.

Abby: Always and till the end of time, my cake twin.

Setting down my phone, I open my iPad and work on my lesson for tomorrow's Spanish class. Before it's time to wake Hayden, I search out fencing clubs in Manhattan, since she told me today she wants to try the sport. When I call one, the head fencing instructor tells me that five is a bit young, but a trial lesson to see if Hayden can focus well enough at her age would be fine. I schedule an introductory session for her in a few days.

Then I rouse her from bed, and once she sheds the remnants of sleep, she proceeds to crush me in a vicious game of Chutes and Ladders before I destroy her in Sorry. We head to the third floor of the building to find Madison, but she's not home. I text Madison's nanny, and she tells me they're in the park, but to please return in the evening. I reply with an emoticon of a fox giving a thumbs up.

Back upstairs, I make edamame and rice for Hayden's dinner, and when she finishes eating, the sound of the key in the lock sends my heart soaring. As I turn to meet Simon's gaze, my heart beats so mercilessly fast, I swear it's going to fly out of my chest.

I want to lock my dumb heart in a cage.

I swallow, wave faintly, and manage a simple hello, while Hayden sets a new land-speed record, racing over to him and jumping in his arms. He gives her the biggest hug in the universe, and damn, if the sight of that—his strong, sturdy arms wrapped around the little girl who worships him—doesn't melt me, I don't know what will. Butterflies take off in my stomach, and I want to tell them to settle down, but the feeling is such a wonderful one that I let myself exist with it a little longer.

"Tell me about your day," he says, his voice bright and happy as he sets her down.

Hayden tells him to wait just one teeny second so she can give him something, then runs to her room, presumably, to fetch the bamboo plant.

From the kitchen, I chime in, "I scheduled a fencing lesson for her."

The corners of his lips curve up. "You did?"

"She said she wanted to try it. I thought it would be okay to just go ahead and set it up. I researched the club and everything." I share what the instructor said about her being young. "But she has good focus when she wants, so I think it'll be great for her."

His smile widens. "Thank you, Abby. I really appreciate it."

"And I set it up for early evening, since sometimes you can get away then," I continue from my post in the kitchen. "And I know you like to go with her the first time she tries new activities. It's near your office."

His grin is supersized now. "That's fantastic. Yes, I would love to go. Thank you again," he says, and he takes a step into the kitchen area. For a moment, time stops when he looks at me. I want to tell him I can't pretend, that it's terribly hard, especially this very second, with him so damn handsome in his black slacks and dark blue shirt, the cuffs rolled up, showing off his forearms.

God, his forearms.

My eyes roam up his body, settling on his face, and the five o'clock shadow stubble that I now know feels fantastic against my chin when he kisses me. A hot flare bursts in my chest at the memory, swooping through me. My knees go weak, and I grip the counter to steady myself.

But then, I remember the weirdness in the cab. How he acted. How we agreed to pretend it never happened.

He raises an eyebrow. "You okay?"

I blink and nod, fighting off every instinct that tells me to launch myself at him.

Hayden's footsteps crash across the living room, breaking the spell of the moment. *Thank the Lord.*

"Look!"

She thrusts the bamboo plant at her father. "It's for luck. Good luck, Daddy. In your business deal. You're a superstar!"

I turn away from them. If I watch him interact with his daughter any more, my ovaries will explode. I will turn into a swoony mess of hormones. Grabbing the plates from the counter to put in the sink, I call out, "Did you want to do that French practice now?"

"That would be great."

He retrieves the jungle coloring book I bought for Hayden from the living room and settles her at the little dinosaur table, while we pull up stools at the island counter in the kitchen. I put on my tutor blinders, doing my best to focus on teaching him words and phrases, rather than staring longingly at those lips I want to kiss, those arms I want to touch, or those eyes I want to get lost in.

I slide my finger across the iPad screen, opening the language app. "Now where did we leave off?" I scroll to a section of the app that covers business terms. "Let's see. Last time I saw you, we worked on . . ."

I freeze as the awareness of my own running commentary slams into me.

Well, Abby, we left off with my hands in your hair, and your lips crushed to mine, and then all the awkwardness in the world rained down, and will you please forgive me, and let me go down on you later when we're alone? Only I have no idea if we can be alone, but this is a fantasy so, hey, we're alone, and I'm fucking crazy about you, too.

I turn to face him and words spill out. "I meant, in our sessions. Where did we leave off in our tutoring sessions? Not anything else," I add quickly, each clarification tumbling onto the next, as if I'm autocorrecting what I pretended he said in my head.

Good Lord.

A faint smile plays on his lips. "I knew what you meant," he says softly.

If he knows what I meant, does he have any clue what's going on inside me? I wonder if I'm truly as bad as Harper says I am at keeping my feelings hidden, and if he can read my mind and my heart.

Clearly there's only one option for me right now. Speak in tongues. I repeat what he just said, but in French. *I knew what you meant.* Like that, we are teacher and student, not woman and man, not nanny and single father.

A fast learner, Simon is rattling off new phrases with alacrity at the end of the hour. Then, he shows me an email from Gabriel about the man's business expansion plans and needs, including how they want to build out a commercial kitchen.

I raise an eyebrow and point at the screen. "You're not going to have to discuss all of *that* with him in French, are you? Cabinetry and kitchens on top of business terms?"

It's one thing to pick up key words and phrases; it's entirely another skill to conduct business in a new language.

He laughs lightly. "I just want to do a better job chatting with his business partners, like Eduardo. I want to impress them. I have a dinner with him this weekend, and I hope to get closer to sealing the deal."

An idea pops into my head. "Wait," I say slowly, returning to the email and running my finger across the note. "He says here that he's looking to hire a contractor for the kitchen."

Simon nods. "Yeah?"

A smile spreads on my face. "I know someone. Harper's fiancé's twin brother is a carpenter. Wyatt Hammer. He specializes in kitchens. Want me to connect you two? That might really impress these guys. They might not know the Manhattan contractors and carpenters yet, and to have a recommendation . . ."

The expression on Simon's face tells me all I need to know. He beams. "I would love that, Abby. Thank you. Especially since Wyatt Hammer is pretty much the perfect name for a carpenter."

It's my turn to laugh, and it feels good to be back to normal with Simon. "It is. And you're learning quickly.

I'm proud of you," I say, and I give myself a mental pat on the back for a different reason. Right now I'm killing it as the super-professional nanny-slash-tutor.

Hayden skips over to us and gives me a page with a pink giraffe and her father a bright orange hippo.

"Am I a hippo?" he asks curiously.

"Hippos are cute," Hayden declares, then turns to me for corroboration. "Aren't they, Abby?"

"Hippos are awesome," I say.

"So are giraffes," Simon says, flashing me a quick smile. Tingles rush over my skin. Damn if I'm not hopelessly gone for him if a comment about giraffes melts me.

But before this jungle talk can turn into some strange sort of new innuendo, Hayden tugs on his sleeve. "Can we go see Madison? They're supposed to be home now."

"Let's do it."

"I'll clean up while you're gone," I offer. "I need to finish the dishes."

Simon waves me off. "You don't have to. I can do them later."

"I don't mind." It's my job, and I won't let him go easy on me.

As I clean, my mind goes blank, focusing on the simple task of washing. Five minutes later, the plates are drying in the rack, and I wipe my hands on a dishtowel. There. This whole day has proven we can do this. We can return to the time before he kissed me and flipped my world upside-down.

When I turn around, Simon has returned.

Alone.

CHAPTER FIFTEEN

Abby

"Where's Hayden?" My voice wobbles.

Simon walks into the kitchen. "She's down at Madison's. They made a powerful case for watching an episode of some show where horses turn into fairies with magical powers like Greek gods."

I arch a skeptical brow.

He gives a one-shouldered shrug. "It makes no sense to me, either, but they like it, and she doesn't seem tired, so . . ." He drops a hand on the kitchen island. We're maybe two or three feet apart, and already the air between us is thick with tension. With hippos and giraffes. That are awesome and cute.

Or maybe it's all in my mind.

Or it's my nerves, skating over my skin, racing through my blood.

"I guess I should go. I'm all done cleaning up." My voice sounds pinched, and I know it's because I'm a jumble right now.

"Abby," he says, low but firm.

I swallow. "Yes?"

"I want to talk to you about the other day." He sounds so serious.

All of a sudden, the weight of my mistake crashes down. "Are you firing me?" I blurt out.

His jaw drops. "What?"

"I'm sorry," I say, and the wild anxieties consume me once more. "I love this job, and I love working with Hayden, and I didn't mean to jeopardize it by . . ."

By making out with you? By touching you? By murmuring your name when you kissed me senseless in the cab, and would you please just do it again?

He steps closer. My stomach makes like a skydiver.

"You did not jeopardize a thing. I'm not firing you. I promise." His blue eyes are locked to mine. "I hope I didn't make you uncomfortable. And I hope I didn't lose you, either. You're so good at what you do, and I value your skills so much. You're great with Hayden, and I don't want to mess that up. I'm sorry for crossing the line."

I shake my head. "It's okay. I crossed it, too."

He licks his lips. "And I really appreciated you inviting me out with your friends. I wanted to go, but I didn't want to mess up your night. I didn't want to make you uncomfortable."

A grin threatens to take over my face because my heart soars. I thought he was turning me down. Instead, he was thinking of me. "You wouldn't have messed it up."

"I wouldn't have?"

"No." I latch onto Harper's advice. *Talk to him.* "I wanted you there."

My breath comes fast, and the hairs on my arms stand on end. We're so near to each other—our words, our voices, our bodies. Everything in me reaches for him.

"I'm glad," he whispers.

"And you don't make me uncomfortable. I promise."

He doesn't say anything in response. Just nods. I press my teeth into my lips. My back is against the sink, and he's standing so close I can smell him. The faint scent of his soap intoxicates me. He must have gone to the gym after work and taken a shower, and oh God, now I'm imagining him naked in the shower, soaping up his strong body. I go up in flames.

"What happened in the cab was"—he pauses, as if he's searching for the right word—"crazy." But the way he says it in a voice full of longing doesn't sound like crazy-bad. It sounds like . . .

"Crazy-good," I supply.

He nods. "So good," he whispers, and inches closer.

"It was *so* good," I echo, my voice breathy, full of this potent need for him.

He stares at me, his eyes brimming with heat. I exhale, and my lips part slightly. He's looking at my mouth now, and I'm burning all over.

We collide.

His hands are in my hair, and his lips crush mine. My fingers race up his shirt and around his neck. I pull him against me, his strong, hard body aligned with mine. His erection presses against my belly, and the realization that he's already hard thrills me. Sparks fly through me as I register *how* hard he is, and my God, I want him. I want to feel him slide into me, I want to take him deep into my body. I want him to know what he does to me, too—that I'm as turned on as he is, and I can't stop kissing him.

His big hands curl around my head, and I moan into his mouth. I love how much bigger he is than I am—taller, broader, stronger. He meets every primal desire I have to be taken. I want this man to consume me. I want to be under him, I want to be pinned by him—I want the full weight of him moving over me.

His lips are demanding, coaxing out more and more kisses from me. More murmurs, more sighs. As I arch into him, he groans, rough and husky.

Then, he breaks the kiss.

"This is bad," he says firmly, his breath coming heavily. But then, he's not so certain at all. "Is this bad?"

"Yes," I answer quickly. "It's bad. But it's so good."

"God, it's so good," he rasps, then devours my lips again. I unlace my hands from his neck, traveling down his chest, exploring the outline of his pecs, then his abs. I gasp. They're so firm, so strong, and I want to rip off his shirt and trace the grooves with my fingers.

He bends his head to my neck and blazes a trail of kisses down to my collarbone, tugging at my shirt. My wandering hands make their way to his ass, and I grab his rear, yanking him closer. Letting him know where I want him. Between my legs. But I'm too short.

He's quick, though. In a second, he lifts me up onto the counter, and I open my legs for him and jerk him closer. A pulse beats between my thighs, a deep and intense desire to have him inside my body. I rub against him, lust overcoming me.

He breathes out hard, panting. "You feel amazing."

"So do you." Then, because I'm in a brazen mood, I add, "I'm so turned on."

"Yeah?" An eyebrow rises, like he wants more, like he's inviting me to give him proof.

I want him to do something about this exquisite ache between my legs. I want him to touch me intimately. I'm desperate. Letting go of his deliciously firm ass, I reach for his hand, untangling it from my hair. I bring his palm to my belly and place his hand against my shirt, then gently guide him lower.

His eyes float closed, and he moans. "Abby," he mutters as his fingers travel south, down to the waistband of my skirt.

"Yes," I say, letting him know to keep going.

His shoulders rise and fall as his hand explores farther down my thigh, then he fingers the hem of my skirt. "Is this okay?"

I love that he asks. I love that he's worried. Most of all, I love that he's going to touch me anyway. "Yes. It's more than okay. I want it. I want you."

"God, I want you so much," he says on a moan as his hand tiptoes up my bare thigh. He's inches away from my center, and his breath seizes up as he nears my panties. "You're so wet," he says before he even touches me. His voice is full of a sexy kind of wonder.

I manage a tiny grin. "It's what you do to me." Then I add, "You're a good lubricant."

He laughs lightly. "Better than water." Then his eyes darken as he stares at me. "My beautiful Abby. Let me take care of this for you," he says, his eyes holding mine hostage as I nod several times, giving him my yes over and over and over.

He grips my hip. With his free hand, his fingers glide across the cotton panel of my panties, already soaked through. "So damn wet," he murmurs.

I push against his fingers, seeking contact, seeking his touch. He answers my need, dipping his hand inside my underwear then sliding his fingers through all my wetness.

I cry out.

He groans.

It's perfect, our twin reactions. We are so in sync. I rock my hips into his hand as he strokes me.

He rubs circles where I want him most, and I moan and sigh and murmur. My words become a series of *oh God*, and *please*, and *more*. He picks up the pace, gliding his fingers faster over me while his lips kiss my neck, my ear. "You feel so fucking good," he says in a throaty rumble.

"So do you," I murmur and tug him closer, needing to feel the outline of his erection. He pushes his hard-on against my thigh with unhurried thrusts, as his hand works some kind of dirty magic between my legs. I rock into his touch, my breath coming faster. He thrusts a finger inside me, then one more, and I nearly scream in pleasure.

"Oh God, oh God, oh God," I murmur as he fucks me with his fingers, thrusting deep inside, rubbing against my clit, all while he kisses my neck and whispers sweet nothings in my ear.

Thought about this so many times.

Want you so much.

Dreamed about making you come.

Pleasure bursts through me and claws at my skin from his words. My belly tightens as I ride his hand, my hips going wild on him.

"Yes," he groans. "I want you to come so badly."

Moans and noises fall from my lips as my vision blurs, and the tension in me hits a new high. Then all at once, it bursts, shattering in a million tiny explosions as I come hard on his hand right there in his kitchen.

Crying out his name. Panting like a wild woman. Holding tight to this man.

When at last I open my eyes, he's grinning dopily at me. "You're so beautiful when you let go."

I smile back at him. I have no clue what's going on with us, but we're both clearly riding a pleasure high right now.

I inhale deeply and reach a hand to his erection, running my palm over it. "Do we have time? Can I?"

He glances at the clock. "I need to get her in ten more minutes," he says, and before he can say any more, my busy fingers work open his zipper, and my palm is on his hard-on, feeling him through his boxer briefs. He's hot and big, and my mouth waters as I stroke the outline of his length.

He shudders as I touch him through the fabric. I love how hard he is, but this isn't enough. I need to feel him fully—my skin against his bare skin. I dip my fingers inside his briefs and wrap a hand around his erection, and we both groan loudly. I think I'm even louder touching him than I was when I came, because he's thick and long, and he fucking loves being touched by me. The sounds he makes as I stroke him are so damn sexy—low, husky, masculine groans of pleasure.

"Abby," he moans, his eyes squeezing shut as he rocks into my hand.

I smile wickedly even though he can't see me. I'm so damn thrilled that he's lost in me like I am in him. He pushes forward, and I work my hand up and down his hard length, savoring the smooth feel of him. "I want to taste you," I say, and I don't whisper it. I don't murmur. I'm bold and confident, because that's how I am with this man I want.

His eyes snap open. They're glossy, full of lust. And just as I'm sure he's about to push his jeans to the floor so my mouth can get to know him better, he shakes his head and cups my cheeks. "I'm dying to taste you. I can't stop thinking about it. Would you let me? Just a taste, and then . . ."

I don't know what comes after the *then*, but I can't say no to that request. Not after the way he asked. Not after my panties grow even more damp from his words. Alone in my bed at night, my knees have fallen open as I've dreamed of his lips.

"Yes."

Gently, he lifts me off the counter and sets me on my feet. Then he drops to his knees on the tile of his kitchen, pushes my cotton skirt to my waist, and pulls down my panties to my ankles. I step out of them. I should be cautious but endorphins have turned off my logical brain. I'm comprised solely of my carnal self.

"So fucking beautiful," he says, adoringly. He runs his hands up the bare flesh of my thighs, kissing my legs with such reverence that I want to cry out in pleasure from that alone. This man is too much. He's amazing. He's incredible. And he's kissing me where I want him most.

My world turns electric as his tongue slides across me. My knees buckle, and he grips my legs, holding me as I grab his head, threading my fingers through his thick hair.

"*Simon*," I gasp as he strokes me with his tongue.

I'm lit up, white-hot from this heavenly pleasure as he licks and sucks and kisses. And he's not quiet, either. He moans and murmurs as he consumes me, and those sounds from him send a new wave of pleasure up and down my body.

"That's more than a taste," I tease as he presses his mouth hard to me.

"You taste so good I can't stop," he murmurs then returns to my slick heat, lapping me up, licking my clit, and kissing me until my world is turned inside out with pleasure.

I grapple at his hair, pull him closer, and rock into his face until I reach that crest once more, flying off as I climax again. I hold nothing back. I'm loud and wild, and I grip his head hard until I come down.

Soon, he rises and wraps his arms around me. "I've wanted to do that for so long."

"Let me do that to you," I say, in a sexy purr.

A groan escapes his lips. "Don't think I'm not tempted. Immensely tempted. But I need to be downstairs in two minutes."

"I'm guessing that's probably not enough time for me to blow your mind," I say playfully.

He smiles at me, a sweet, sexy grin.

"It's not fair that you didn't get to come," I say.

He drops a kiss to my forehead. "It's completely fair, since I was able to do that to you twice." Then he sighs, and his tone is full of longing. "What am I going to do with you?"

"I don't know. I don't have a clue." But in one minute, he needs to pick up his daughter. I separate. That's the reality, and that's not something we can toy with. "You need to get Hayden, and I should go, too."

"We'll talk later?"

I nod, and then he leaves. I gather my things in a flurry, pulling on my panties and rushing out of my place of employment, flush from two epic orgasms, courtesy of my boss.

Who I'm falling into some kind of madness with.

CHAPTER SIXTEEN

Simon

I don't have any more answers that night when I flop into bed on top of my covers. My daughter is sound asleep, and I grab a pen from the nightstand, twirling it between my thumb and forefinger, back and forth.

I set it down, reach for my phone, and slide my index finger over the lock code. I draw a sharp breath, and toss it on the bed. I park my hands behind my head, trying to navigate this path with Abby, like I evaluate business deals. In this case, each step is fraught with potholes.

Risking her job.

Hurting Hayden.

Losing someone Hayden adores.

Becoming a cliché.

A darkness slides through my veins as that word echoes in my head. *Cliché.*

Like I called Miriam when she cheated with her co-worker. Like I became by working too much. Even though I cut back on the relentless pace of deal-making, I can still negotiate and navigate with the best of them. I can turn a small wad of money into a pot of gold. I can sniff out opportunity, and I can smell trouble, too.

But here, I can't decide which path is riskier, because every second I spend with Abby makes me want more of her. Every laugh, every comment—every thing she says or does. The more I have of Abby, the more I want.

I stretch my arm for the phone, giving in.

Maybe if I were stronger I'd sort this out with Kristy or Tyler. I'd write up a list of pros and cons, like a business deal.

But this isn't fucking business. It's my heart, and that damn persistent organ wants her. Other organs do, too. As I click on her name in my contacts, I rationalize that maybe I'm sorting this out with the one person I *should* be talking to. Because that's what I learned tonight—this thing between us is real, and it's combustible. It wasn't a one-time incident. It has the potential to flare more brightly each time.

I start with a simple hello.

Simon: Hi

Abby: Hi

Simon: Tonight was . . . amazing.

Abby: I think I'm still glowing.

Simon: You are so beautiful. So sensual.

Abby: You make me feel that way. I love it when you touch me.

Well, hello there, dirty texting.

I didn't expect to head in this direction so quickly, but then, that seems to be what we do lately. As I stare at her words, I burn up all over. I'm hard as a rock. She's so direct, so forward, and it reels me in.

Simon: I can't get enough of touching you. Of kissing you. Of tasting you. When I close my eyes, I swear you're with me. I can smell you. It's intoxicating.

Abby: You should know it's the same for me. Those twenty minutes in your kitchen are on repeat in my head. Like I DVR'd them and keep hitting replay.

I crack up at her description.

Simon: I want access to your DVR. I'd like to binge watch that show.

Abby: What are you doing right now?

Simon: Lying in bed, in my T-shirt and boxers, texting you. You?

Abby: Lying in bed, in a tank top and panties, texting you.

I groan at the image. My dick hardens even more, and I skim my hand lightly over my erection.

Simon: If I were there, I wouldn't be able to keep my hands off you. But I think we've established I'm terrible at resisting you.

Abby: I'm terrible at making you stop. Because it feels so good when you don't stop. I'm shuddering as I remember what you did to me.

I breathe out hard, recalling her sounds, her whimpers, and her noises.

Simon: I'm thinking of it now, too. Loved every second of everything. I want to do it all again.

Abby: I want it, too, but didn't we say it was bad? (Well, good but bad!)

Simon: I should know, but I lose all sense of reason when I'm near you.

Abby: I felt like you were lost in me tonight when I touched you. And I loved that.

Simon: God, I was. I'm wishing you were here.

Abby: What would you do?

Simon: Kiss you again. Take you to my bed. Undress you. Is that too much?

Abby: I want that. I want all of that. It's not too much. Right now, it feels like it's not enough.

Simon: You feel incredible in my arms. But you have to know there's so much more to this for me. It's so much deeper.

Abby: I know . . . Trust me . . . I know . . . It's the same for me.

Simon: But that's the hardest thing . . . I feel so much for you, and when I see you, I want to take you in my arms. I don't know how to be in the same room with you and NOT want to touch you.

Abby: That is indeed THE HARDEST THING. :)

Simon: Ha! Walked right into that one.

Abby: You sure did. But the issue remains. Should we try to stop? To prove we can or something? Like the feats of strength from George's Festivus on *Seinfeld*? And if you don't know that episode, I don't know that we should even talk again. :)

Simon: As if I don't know about a Festivus for the rest of us.

Abby: Good. Keep talking . . .

Simon: But how do you know Festivus? The show ended when you were...wait, don't even tell me how young you were when it ended.

Abby: Please. I WAS EIGHT WHEN IT ENDED, WHICH MEANS YOU WERE SIXTEEN, AND THAT IS JUST FINE WITH ME! Also, I watched Seinfeld reruns in college.

Simon: Confession—I still watch Seinfeld reruns. Anyway, resisting you sounds like an insane challenge. I've always enjoyed a good challenge, though.

Abby: A good, hard challenge. Incidentally, thanks for being so selfish and batting my hand away from something good and hard I was enjoying.

Now, I crack up, laughing even as I'm royally fucking turned on.

Simon: Oh, Abby. If memory serves, you didn't mind at all when I got down on my knees and made you come so fucking hard again on my lips.

Abby: *combusts from the hotness of the memory*

Simon: *wonders when I can do that to you again*

Abby: Um, by the way, how is this conversation helping us prove our devotion to Festivus?

Simon: Do you want to stop? To prove we can?

Abby: It's not that I want to. I just think we need to know we can work together and not rip off each other's clothes every second.

Simon: Occupational hazard and all.

Abby: But one best avoided.

Simon: Yes. If we can. By the way, you should check out the American Bald Eagle Association's collection of pictures from the day. You'll love them.

I grin, confident she'll be enthralled with the shots of the two bald eagles rearranging branches in the nest to build it up and prevent the little ones from falling out. Three minutes later, she replies.

Abby: You're right. I do love them. Madly.

I know her. I know this woman.

CHAPTER SEVENTEEN

Simon

It's sort of like withdrawal.

The next day, I spend my morning with Hayden, taking her to story time at An Open Book, our favorite bookstore on the Upper West Side. Then for lunch, she decides to try garlic fries, even though I warn her that garlic is not her friend. But hey, we all have to learn in our own way.

When we return home, I don't even have to say *I told you so*. She launches a full-scale attack on her breath with her strawberry toothpaste.

Abby arrives while Hayden's in the bathroom. We say hello. Chastely. But I'm not ashamed to say my stomach flips when I see her. This woman—she's so gorgeous, and she rocks a sundress. The one she wears today is light blue. A little peach summer sweater is on her shoulders.

"How was Spanish class this morning? Was that new student still giving you a hard time?" I ask as she sets her purse on the coffee table.

She tilts her head, surprised. "You knew I had a Spanish class?"

I tug on my earlobe. "Yes. I'm a good listener. And you told me about the new guy who kept insisting Google Translate was all he needed." I admit it. I'm trying blatantly to impress her.

Judging from the appreciative rise of her eyebrows, I've succeeded. "Yes," she says, rolling her eyes. "His employer sent him to the class, but he thought he didn't need it. Until I told him about the festival of turnip greens."

I rub my hands together. "Tell me about turnip greens."

She scans the living room. "Where's Hayden?"

"Conducting a full decontamination on her teeth. She had garlic for lunch."

Abby crinkles her nose. "I detest garlic. I once tried to start a petition to have it removed."

"Removed from . . . the world?"

"Yes. I was fourteen and quite idealistic. I kissed a boy after eating garlic pizza, and he told me my breath was gross. So I started an online petition."

That's just too adorable. "Against the boy? Or against the vegetable?"

She parks her hands on her hips. "The vegetable, of course."

"Did you get any signatures?"

She nods vigorously. "My God, the anti-garlic contingent is powerful. There are tons of people around the world who think it's nature's curse. Along with zucchini." She shudders. "There's no reason for zucchini to exist. Or at least, the oversize version of it when someone grows it in a garden and it gets too big."

One corner of my lips quirks up. "You are a perfect woman. I, too, believe in the abolition of garlic and gigantic zucchini."

She smiles back at me. And yes, it's just garlic and a too-big vegetable, but it's also so much more. It's an acknowledgement that we have these little things—and so many big things, too—in common.

I make a rolling gesture to remind her to keep telling the story. "The turnip greens. That's the veggie under discussion. Go on."

She peers down the hallway, then lowers her voice. "I told him the story of the culinary festival in a Galician town in northwest Spain. It was meant to celebrate the *grelo,* a leafy green vegetable, but in fact the small town was marketing it in a very different way thanks to Google Translate. Instead, the small town invited its residents and visitors alike to a . . ." Abby stops, collects herself, then blurts out, "A clitoris festival."

A deep belly laugh climbs through me, then I fix on a serious expression. "I can't say I'd mind attending such an event. That is, if you invited me."

"Anyway, the festival holds tastings and awards for the best *grelos,*" she says, punctuating those last two words with naughty panache. "According to its marketing, the clitoris is one of the typical products of Galician cuisine, and a star of its local gastronomy."

I smirk. "I've always thought the clitoris should be the star of any show it's in."

She swats my arm. "See? You would probably find Google Translate acceptable."

I shake my head. "Never. Not when I could have a teacher like you. By the way, did the student understand the value of a teacher thanks to the clitoris lesson?"

Abby laughs. "I do believe he's been converted."

The clitoris conversation halts when Hayden rushes out of her room, racing through the hall. She stops short at my feet, lifts her chin, and breathes out hard.

"So much better," I tell her, then I leave my two favorite people in the world behind as I head to the office.

* * *

When I return home in the evening, we say goodbye.

Chastely.

But I whisper in her ear, "I'd kiss you even if you tasted like garlic."

She trembles, then she leaves.

* * *

Abby

Later that night, the email notification flashes on my phone. As I sink down onto my couch, I grab my cell, and my heart skips a beat when I see the note is from Simon.

> I thought you might like to know I started an online petition tonight. It's to recall all forms of zucchini, with a special provision to ban the use of zucchini as a present. I've titled it: "Zucchini is not a gift. It's a punishment." Let's hope these efforts can halt the nefarious habit of neighbors with gardens from trying to unload their oversize, tasteless vegetables under the guise of gifts. Also, zucchini bread? It too is outlawed in this provision.
>
> By the way, you looked stunning today in that blue dress. I'm confident, though, that as good as it looks on you, it would look ten thousand times better taken off you by me.

Crossing my legs at the ankles, I laugh at the same time he turns me on. I've started to tap out a reply when another envelope icon appears.

His name on my phone screen sends a flurry of shivers down my spine.

Also, did you know that the French phrase "*Se taper le cul par terre*" means to laugh uproariously? You probably did. Funnily enough, Google Translate will tell you it means "ass banging on the floor." I believe this gives new meaning to the phrase "laugh my ass off." It's also a great reminder of the value of language teachers.

By the way, you're so much hotter than Google Translate. That's another benefit of you as a teacher. Though, come to think of it, if any of your students look at you the way I do, I might have to go caveman on them.

My response is simple. I shoot him back a note saying: **Is Google Translate hot???**

Then I ring him. It's after ten, and I know Hayden is sound asleep. "So you have it bad for your teacher?" I say when he answers.

He laughs, a rich, deep sound. But what he says next isn't funny. It's dirty and makes a pulse beat between my legs.

* * *

Simon

I close the door to my bedroom, ensuring privacy. Then, with the phone pressed close to my ear and my filthy imagination already firing on all cylinders, I answer her question.

"I want to bend my teacher over the desk."

Her breath hitches. "Naughty student."

I sink down on my bed, picturing perfectly what I want to do to her. "Hike up your skirt. Pull down your panties."

"I like this image," she says breathily. "Would you pin my wrists over my head then?"

I groan appreciatively, loving the image she evokes. "You'd like that, wouldn't you?"

"I would." Her voice is a purr, and I can see her now—on her couch, her hand drifting down her belly. And just like that, my dick refuses to be ignored.

I skim a hand over my erection. "I'm going to file that piece of intel safely away and use it someday soon."

"I look forward to that someday." She's quiet for a moment, then her voice is soft. "You really thought about my dress today?"

"This surprises you? Was there something unclear about the obscene levels of desire I have for you?"

She laughs lightly. "No. But tell me. Was I wearing anything under the dress when you took it off?"

I like where this is going even more, and I push my briefs down, wrapping a hand around my shaft. "Black lace panties. Matching bra. I stripped them off then kissed you all over, and you melted when I touched you."

"I do melt when you touch me."

"And now? Are you melting now?" I ask, because I'm fucking burning up all over as I touch myself.

"I'm on fire." She gasps, and the sound lingers so seductively.

"Did you just touch yourself?"

"Yes, and I'm picturing you."

All I can see right now is Abby, naked, her back arched, her hand moving faster between her legs. It's the most arousing image my brain has ever had the good sense to create. "And what am I doing to you?"

She doesn't answer right away. Drawing a sexy breath, she says, "I'm unzipping your jeans."

I'm silent for a few seconds, adjusting to the new direction. I figured she'd detail a scenario of me burying my face between her legs, and hell, if that isn't my favorite thing to get off to. But this is insanely hot, and my fist is already moving up and down my erection as she adds to her fantasy. "I want to do that to you. I want to get on my knees for you."

Oh, fuck. All the blood in my body goes straight to my dick. My breathing grows louder as she tells me how she wants to slide her hand into my boxers, push them down, then touch, stroke, and taste. Her voice and the pictures she paints send me into a tailspin, and I can't get enough of her words. Then she adds, "I'll lick and kiss, and then wrap my lips around you."

I'm close, so fucking close. My voice is husky, thick with lust as my fist flies faster. "I want to see that, Abby. I want to curl my fingers around your head and watch you do that to me."

"I'll take you in all the way." Her breath comes in harsh pants.

"Fuck. I can't get enough of you."

She moans. "I can't get enough, either. I want all of you. I want to taste you in my mouth."

Then words are pointless as our noises become the only soundtrack. She cries out, and I recognize the pitch now, and how it means she's tipping over the edge. The pleasure in me skyrockets. I picture her on the other side of the park, her fingers between her legs, sending herself soaring. That image blazes in front of me, and the tension in my body tightens, then snaps. My release is powerful, but over far too soon as I groan her name into the phone, and she does the same for me.

My body is still buzzing a minute later after I clean up. "So if resisting phone sex is one of the feats of strength, we just failed miserably."

"We sure did."

"And I don't regret it at all."

"Nor do I," she says, and then we talk for another hour, and it has nothing to do with sex.

We talk about our least favorite vegetables, and our most favorite fruit, and we agree that cottage cheese is the devil, and wonder how Brussels sprouts somehow tricked everyone into believing it was a cool food.

She tells me she wants to take a trapeze lesson someday, but that I still have to teach her pool, and I tell her I'd love to, especially since she's helped me so much with French. I learn she volunteers for a local literacy program, and I tell her about my plans to run a 10K for a children's hospital charity at the end of this summer.

"I hate running with a passion, but I'll cheer you on," she says.

"I'd like that."

When I say goodbye, it feels like that might happen, and that she'd be there at the finish line, waiting for me.

CHAPTER EIGHTEEN

Abby

The next day, Hayden decides she wants to learn French just like her dad. As we traipse around the city, I teach her the words for swing, and store, and chocolate-chip cookie.

As the evening draws near, we catch the subway to the Village, making our way to the restaurant on Christopher Street where Simon is meeting Nick's twin brother about an estimate. Simon asked me to hand off Hayden here since he has plans tonight to take her to a movie in nearby Chelsea.

The funny thing is, when he told me, I nearly asked if I could join them. I found myself wanting to go to the movies with the two of them, grab a bag of kettle corn, and accidentally brush fingers with Simon as we reached for a handful at the same time.

My stomach pirouettes at the possibility. I grip Hayden's little hand tighter, focusing on her, not her father.

It's not easy.

It's really hard.

But I award myself another gold medal, this time in the One City Block Walk Without Thinking of Simon.

When we reach the restaurant site, I push open the door, and Hayden flies inside and throws her arms around her dad. "Daddy! My lesson was so fun! Abby is teaching me French too! *Bonjour*!"

"*Bon soir, ma chérie*," he says as he scoops her up in his arms, and my heart soars as he speaks to her in French. "I think that's great, sweet pea. Will you tell me more the second I'm done?"

Hayden nods and gives him a big kiss on the cheek, then snuggles closer. *Skyrocket* is the more apropos verb now, because my damn heart launches itself into the stratosphere when he turns and looks at me.

The breath flees my chest.

His eyes sparkle like he has a secret. Like *we* have a secret. And we do. How we feel about each other. Even with all this space between us, and all the people here, I swear I'm the only one he sees.

"Hey Abby," he says, and I hear something new in his voice. Something stronger, and softer, too. Like I'm the person—besides his little princess—that he most wants to see at the end of his day.

"Hi," I say, and in that one word, and how it falls from my lips, he has to know it's the same way for me.

As I head to the door, I feel his eyes on me the whole time. That's where I want them. I want him to be looking at me, longing for me, falling for me.

Because I'm in so deep with him.

Simon

That night, our language lesson is on the phone as she helps me prep for the dinner this weekend. She teaches me how to ask important questions about wine. I ask her if wine makes her frisky.

"Don't you already know? I had a few glasses before I jumped you at the zebra movie."

"Ah, I wasn't sure if it was me, or the stripes, or the wine."

"All three," she says, then instructs me on how to compliment the chef on the food.

I repeat her words, and then I compliment her on how she tastes better than dessert.

"Oh stop," she says shyly, and I can hear the blush in her voice. "And next time it's my turn with you."

Can't argue with that. Especially since she wants a next time. Maybe we're not resisting each other. Maybe it's just semantics when we say phone sex isn't the same as ripping each other's clothes off.

But even so, we've managed a hands-off week. And more than that, we're proving something vitally important —how much more there is to us than mere attraction.

As the night rolls to its end, I remind her that it's my turn to teach her. "Turns out Hayden has a birthday party for two hours tomorrow night. Any chance I can take you out to a pool hall and teach you to play, like I promised?"

"As long as you do that thing where you line up behind me and show me how to make the shot."

And that's precisely what I do the next night. She leans forward on the table, lining up her shot, peering at the orange ball as she pulls back the wooden stick.

"Like this?" she asks over her shoulder.

"Just like that."

I crowd in behind her, pressing my body against her, positioning the cue between her fingers. She murmurs, and I nip her shoulder blade. My mind is awash in dirty images courtesy of this position, and my God, how I want her like this, bent over, her arms braced on the green felt. My dick throbs in my jeans, and I know she can feel my erection against her ass. Her wonderful, lush ass. I push against her, and her breath shudders.

"And then you pull it back like this," I say, showing her as I move the cue.

She leans her head back into me, and I draw in a deep, intoxicating inhalation of her hair. Her coconut scent floods my nostrils and kicks my arousal into overdrive.

"Is this us not ripping each other's clothes off?" she asks, her voice full of heat and fire.

"Yes. Because, sadly, you're still fully dressed. Which seems to be an affront to all my baser instincts."

"I like those instincts," she murmurs.

Setting the stick on the table, she spins around. She's pinned between the pool table and me. Journey plays overhead, and other games continue around us. Right now, I don't give a crap who's here. Not as she loops her arms around my neck.

"I do want to tear off your clothes," she whispers, then drags one hand down the buttons of my white shirt. She plays with the top button, slipping it open.

"Are you actually going to take my clothes off here at a pool hall?" I ask skeptically.

But she ignores the question as she gasps. "Oh my God, I didn't know you had a tattoo."

"Only because you've never gotten my clothes off before."

She slides open another button and rubs her fingers over the ink—a large Celtic circular piece on my pec. "What does it mean?"

"Trust. Trust yourself."

She lifts her face and looks at me. "When did you have it done?"

"When I finished college. It was a reminder to trust my instincts with work and career. But it came to mean other things."

"Like trust your instincts with Miriam?"

Hearing her name isn't a punch in the kidney anymore. It doesn't hurt. That pain is long gone. "I had to rely on my gut. That it was time to go and end the marriage."

"Do you ever regret it ending?"

I shake my head. "No. We were wrong for each other. And I'm not someone who believes you stay together for the kid. My daughter is better off with us apart. I had to trust myself to know that."

She nods her understanding, then tilts her head to the side. "And do you trust yourself with me?"

I chuckle lightly. "Sometimes I do. Sometimes I don't."

"When don't you?"

"Right now." I dip my head to her neck, growling in her ear. "When I want to get the hell out of here and make the most of the thirty minutes we have left, even though we promised to keep our hands to ourselves."

"What if I don't use my hands then?" she asks, her tone flirty.

I wrench back to look at her. "Don't use your hands?"

She runs her finger across her bottom lip. "What if I just use my mouth? Would you trust yourself to enjoy it? Would you trust me to make it good for you? Would you trust us to know it's what we both want?"

My head spins, and I'm dizzy with lust. "What am I going to do with you?"

* * *

Abby

He doesn't take long to devise an answer. The man knows how to get stuff done. He's a dealmaker, a problem solver, and he simply calls a car service he says he knows from his Wall Street days and orders a vehicle, stat. I don't ask why he doesn't use Uber, because ten minutes later the answer is obvious when we climb into a long sleek car.

With a partition.

God bless the old school car service solution.

"Just drive," he tells the man in the black cap.

Simon presses the button for the divider, and in seconds we're alone on the leather seat. Quickly, I unzip his pants and take his erection in my hand.

"You said no hands," he says on a moan.

"I lied. Do you care?"

He grins. "No."

"Good. Then I'm going to the zucchini festival right now."

He cracks up. But then his laughter is swallowed by his groan as I dip my head between his legs. I swirl my tongue over the tip of his erection, and he moans when I make contact. I do, too. The taste of him is heady—masculine and sexy, a little salty, and all addictive. I flick my tongue across him, then down the shaft, and he thrusts up into me.

He groans my name, and I want to play with him, toy with him, but instead I decide to blow his mind. I wrap my lips around him, and then I take him deep. He's hard and thick, and so fucking aroused. I swear he's throbbing in my mouth. He grips my head, tugging me closer.

There's a roughness to him at times. He never hurts me, but it's a good roughness, like he knows sex is better if we're not delicate. He knows it's okay to grab my hair and yank hard, and my God, I hope he knows he won't have to go easy on me when he makes love to me just because he's so much bigger.

When. Not if.

Because I know it'll happen. We are a *fait accompli,* and I don't say that because I'm treating him like the most delicious lollipop. I say it because neither one of us can get enough of the other.

This week was about proving we could pull this off. That we could work without jumping each other. We passed, successfully, keeping it chaste in the home.

We're not at home now, and we're free, so I draw him deep, stretching my lips over him. I'm wildly aroused by going down on him. I love how he tastes, how he feels, and how much he wants me.

"Abby," he groans. His voice is laced with heat and desire. "I want to come in your mouth."

I let go with a wet *pop* to arch an eyebrow and say, "Like there's any place else you'd come?"

I dive back down, and he's closer, thrusting hard, pushing into me and digging his fingers roughly into my hair and against my skull. Breathing is hard, but I'm up to the task, sucking him deep. As he rocks into my mouth and curls his hands around my head, he issues a guttural moan, then a warning. "Coming. Now."

I don't need the warning, and I love how he loses control for me. I savor the taste of his release sliding down my throat.

When I finally break away, the clock mocks me. He needs to get home.

I tell him as much, and that even though I wish the night wasn't ending, I had the best time with him. He smiles like a happy, woozy man as he pulls me closer and kisses my head. "My sweet, sexy Abby. You know I can't resist you."

My smile widens. "I know. And you taste so much better than zucchini."

CHAPTER NINETEEN

Simon

In her white knickers and a fencing jacket a size too big, Hayden adopts the *en garde* stance and waggles her sword.

I lean forward, my palms on my knees, watching intently. Abby brought Hayden here to the fencing club, and I left work to meet them. She's no fencing prodigy. But she's doing her darnedest to keep up in her first lesson.

After Hayden stabs the instructor in the breastbone, he cheers her on. She turns to me, her young eyes lit up and seeking approval.

"Great job," Abby calls out, then waves to my girl.

"Keep it up," I second, then Hayden returns her focus to the lesson.

"She's having a great time," Abby says, bumping her shoulder against mine.

"She is. Think she'll want another lesson?"

Abby shrugs lightly. "Who knows? She likes to try new things, and that's good."

"I can see her testing every sport once. Every instrument once. She'll want to do rock climbing, then piano, then ice skating."

Abby holds up an index finger. "Karate next, and after that it'll be ballet, then saxophone. She'll have to try singing too."

"Let's not forget gymnastics and origami. She'll probably start an origami club in kindergarten."

"That sounds exactly like her."

I turn to face her completely, and my heart sputters. Abby's smile is wide and pretty, and we're sitting together talking about *my* kid, and we're both just *getting*, totally getting, how Hayden ticks. I can't think of anyplace I'd rather be, or any conversation I'd rather have. This woman has burrowed her way into my heart, simply by being herself. I don't honestly know if I can let her go.

"She should try everything," Abby says, her voice softening, quieter now.

"To see what she likes."

Abby nods. "To see what she falls in love with," she adds softly, her golden eyes never straying from mine.

"She'll definitely fall in love with something," I say, my voice matching hers, my heart beating rapidly.

"Like languages."

"Or restaurants."

"Or something else entirely."

"Or someone, someday," I say, barely a whisper.

As the sound of metal hitting metal in a bout surrounds us, I bend closer to her and speak softly near her ear. "I can't stop falling for you."

She shivers, and her eyes float closed momentarily. When they flutter open, she looks at me once more. "I can't, either, Simon."

The way she says my name, sweet and desperate, threads into me. I'm powerless to resist her. I stop fighting it.

No, I don't kiss her again in the fencing club during my daughter's lesson. Instead, I ask her a question. "Hayden's back with her mom this weekend, and I have a dinner with Gabriel and his guys. Would you like to come with me?"

"Because you're not learning French fast enough?" she asks playfully.

"*Oui*," I say with a grin. "But I'd like your company, too."

"Will you pick me up before dinner?"

I nod. "I will."

CHAPTER TWENTY

Abby

"The paella was amazing when I was in Spain," I tell Gabriel from my spot next to him in his gorgeous apartment, where he's cooked us a feast.

He rolls his eyes in pleasure. "It's to-die-for. Never better than in Barcelona."

"But I bet you can make it even tastier," I say, with a playful challenge.

He laughs, and it matches his personality—big, buoyant, sparkly. I can see why Simon wants to work with him. He's charming and amazingly talented, and the dinner he made for us is divine, an incredible red snapper and risotto, as well as roasted artichoke, lightly seasoned.

His partners are easygoing, and Simon was right. They vastly prefer to speak in French. That's what we've been doing, though Gabriel speaks Spanish, too, and as I chat with him we slide back and forth into that language.

"So you learned all your Spanish abroad?" he asks.

I shake my head as I slice a piece of the fish, the knife slipping through like butter. "My mother is from Spain, so I knew enough beforehand, but in the year there I became fluent enough to teach it now. What about you?" I ask as I bring the bite to my mouth.

He tells me he grew up bilingual, speaking French and Portuguese, but then he mastered English in school and Spanish in his travels.

"It's a handy language to know in the food business," he says as he picks up his glass of wine.

"Yes, I suspect it is," I say and catch the gaze briefly of Simon, who's next to me, chatting with Gabriel's colleagues. There are eight of us here at the table. He's held his own through most of the meal, though I weigh in from time to time and translate. When I do, he shoots me the sweetest smile, one that just melts me.

But then, everything he does seems to have that effect on me.

Maybe even more so tonight, with two glasses of wine making my world particularly warm and toasty.

When Eduardo asks a question about the structure of the deal, the crinkle in Simon's forehead tells me he doesn't understand every word, so I chime in with a translation.

"Thank you," he says softly to me, then answers the goateed man.

As he talks, I turn my focus back to the chef.

Gabriel gestures to Simon with his eyes. "You're good for him," he says in a quiet voice.

"You think so?"

"Yes. The two of you are like a perfect team."

A faint blush creeps across my cheeks. "Thank you."

"How long have you worked together? Because he wasn't speaking like this a few weeks ago. Did you help him?"

I beam and nod. "I did."

"He is lucky to have such a good teacher. And a lovely one," he says, then flashes a charming smile.

We chatter on about travel and food, then about the best wines in the world. A few minutes later, I catch my breath when a hand presses against my thigh. Simon's hand. He doesn't even slide it up my leg—he simply rests it on me as he talks. I don't know if it's one of those things he's barely aware of, or something he's intending. But I know this much—I love that he's touching me.

Gabriel raises a glass of wine. "To good food!"

Eduardo nods. "To good deals!" Then he meets my gaze, waiting for me.

"To good matches!" I turn to Simon.

"To all of you," he says, and as the rest of the guests join in with their toasts, Simon slides his palm up a few inches, and I nearly swoon right there at the dinner table.

I love how much he needs me. I love how much he wants me. I love the way he talks to me. I love how he looks tonight, in his gray slacks, a light blue button-down, and no tie.

I love everything about tonight, including this wine, including the company, and including how much I want this dinner to end so that whatever happens next has a chance of beginning.

* * *

The elevator door in Gabriel's building closes with a soft *whoosh*. We're alone, having just said goodbye. Simon presses the button for the lobby then meets my gaze.

"Dinner was amazing." I feel like I'm glowing, from the good food and good company.

"It was, and I'm so glad you were here with me. Thank you."

"It was my pleasure," I say as I smooth a hand over the skirt of my black dress, a knee-length flouncy number with slim straps.

He steps closer as the car chugs downward. Then even closer as he reaches for my arm and runs his finger down the bare skin. Goosebumps rise in his wake, and I shiver.

I swallow, my eyes staying on his the whole time. "How do you think we're doing with the feats of strength?" I ask, my tone laced with the desire that builds in me every second that he looks at me like this—like I'm the answer to his every wish.

"Well, I haven't ripped off your clothes," he says with a wry grin, his blue eyes sparkling as his fingers change directions, heading back up my arm.

"Pity, that."

He raises his hand to my face and runs the back of his fingers over my jawline. I lean into him and sigh contentedly. I feel as if I'm glowing all over, like everything is bright and beautiful in my world.

"Abby," he says, his voice full of tenderness.

"Yes?"

With his free hand he gestures from me to him. "What's happening here?"

My heart squeezes, and my skin heats to supernova levels. I know what he's asking. I know what he's getting at. I want him to say it first, though. "I think you know," I whisper.

He nods and presses the barest of kisses to my lips. I light up everywhere from that sliver-of-a-second of a kiss. My entire body tingles from head to toe. He separates and gazes at me, and sparklers ignite in every cell of my body. I'm a firework, and I'm about to burst in brilliant red jets of light. If he just says what I think he's going to say . . .

He tucks a finger under my chin as the car slows, nearing the lobby. "I do know."

My body hums with hope. "Then tell me," I say, my voice bare, stripped to pure need.

"I will. I'll tell you what's happening to me, and it's this," he says, stopping to take a breath, holding my gaze. "I'm in love with you."

And I swoon. I melt. I burst. I don't know that I've been very good at resisting this man, but I sure as hell know I no longer want to. I'm crazy for him. Looping my hands around his neck, I pull him close. "I'm so in love with you."

"I've been falling in love with you since the day we met," he says, and my heart soars above the earth.

"It's completely the same for me."

He sighs against me, and it's the happiest of sounds. I've done this. I've made this man incandescently happy. I stand up on tiptoe and move my mouth to his ear. "Will you take me to your home and make love to me?"

A shudder moves through his body, and he answers with the sexiest, hungriest *yes*.

CHAPTER TWENTY-ONE

Simon

She walks into my bedroom looking like she belongs.

Not because she struts in like she lives here. But because she owns me. She's claimed a piece of my heart, and now I have the chance to touch her in the most intimate way.

It staggers me.

Watching her run her fingers along the covers of my bed knocks the breath out of me. She's here. In my bedroom. When she turns around, she drops her purse on my bed, brings her hand to the strap on her shoulder, and gives me the most inviting look.

Like she's saying come and get me.

I will. Oh yes, I will.

"Let me do that," I say, closing the distance between us and pushing the slim black strap of her dress down her shoulder, exposing her bare flesh. "Let me undress you."

I bend to her, kissing her, imprinting my lips on her soft, vanilla-scented skin. She murmurs and sighs as her hands loop into my hair. I travel along her collarbone, nipping her lightly with my teeth then kissing the delicate column of her throat. She stretches her neck, exposing more of her skin for me. I kiss up to her ear, bite down on her earlobe, and whisper, "This feels like a dream."

Her hand curls around my head. "It's all real. I assure you."

"So real," I echo as I brush my lips to hers. "I didn't stand a chance of resisting you, Abby. The minute you walked through my door, it's been a battle."

"It's the same for me, I swear," she says, breathless.

I slide the other strap down then bring my hands to her back and work open the zipper. "I've longed for this moment. Dreamed about it," I say as I glide down the metal teeth.

She trembles, and her breath stuttering like that is the sweetest sound. I don't need music. I don't need noise. I want to hear only her—her gasps, her voice, her sighs, mingling with the far-off din of a New York City night.

"Me, too," she says, her breath ghosting over me. "You have no idea."

"No. I have every idea. Because I'm so fucking crazy about you." My entire body burns with desire for her. My bones vibrate with the need to touch her, to take her, to have her. To be as close to this woman as I possibly can be.

I dip my mouth to hers, crushing her lips in a kiss. My brain goes haywire, my veins shooting full of electricity from the way we connect. As I kiss her hard, I tug her dress to her waist, her hips, then down her legs. I barely break the kiss as she steps out of her clothes.

Her fingers race up my shirt, grasping at buttons, undoing them in a flurry. Soon, she spreads open the fabric, running her hands across my chest, tracing the tattoo. I still for a moment, taking in the enormity of this night.

Abby's hands are on my bare skin. She's touching me. She wants me to make love to her, and I'm going to. I'm going to strip the rest of her clothes off, lay her on my bed naked, and slide into her—

Fuck.

The sky falls, and my night crashes down. "I don't have any condoms," I blurt out.

She wiggles her eyebrows. "But I do."

"You do?"

She shrugs sexily. "I was kind of hoping you'd want this. And I didn't want to presume you stocked them, so I did."

"I don't stock them," I say, and don't need to add *no need to*. Obviously, if I don't have them, that's why.

She reaches for her purse, snaps it open, and tosses the wrapper on the bed.

"Only one?" I tease, as I unbutton my pants.

"I have another one. If we need it," she adds as I toe off my shoes and pull off my socks.

"Oh, we'll need it," I say, my voice commanding, strong. "Once with you won't be enough."

I unzip my pants and take them off, tossing them somewhere on the floor.

She breathes out hard as she stares at my boxer briefs

and the outline of my hard-on. Her eyes widen, looking hazy with lust. Good. I like the way she stares. The way she licks her lips. Her eyes shine with desire, and the look in them makes me even harder.

Her hand reaches out, and she presses it against my dick. I groan.

"Fuck, Abby," I mutter as she rubs her palm against me. Her touch is out of this world. I rock into her hand for a few seconds. Then I step back, taking in how utterly stunning she is, clad only in a dark bra and matching lace panties that will be off her in seconds. "You look gorgeous in all this black, but I'm dying to get you into absolutely nothing."

She runs her hands up my chest and whispers, "Strip me."

So I do, unhooking her bra, sliding off her panties, and then admiring her naked beauty. All that creamy skin, those beautiful breasts, her soft belly, her hips, and then, as she sinks back onto my bed, between her legs, where I want to spend the rest of the night.

I strip off my boxers and climb on top of her, skin to warm skin. She moans and arches up into me, and I could slide into her right now. But I want her wild. I want her reckless. I want her out of her mind with pleasure. Making my way down her beautiful body, I kiss her breasts, her belly, her waist. She raises her knees and lets them fall open.

A lust-fueled reverence charges through my body as I run my hands under her thighs, spread her open more, and bury my face between her legs.

She whimpers the second my tongue flicks against her sweet center. My eyes roll back into my head. She tastes exquisite, and she's mine. All mine. As I kiss and lick her wetness, her fingers tangle into my hair, and she moves with me, her hips rocking up, her back arching.

A broken pant falls from her lips, then a plea.

More, please, God, more.

It's so good.

Oh God, it's so good.

Her words ignite me as I devour her. Soon, she turns wilder, frantic and frenzied, her fingers gripping my skull as she grinds against my tongue. She's all over me, her liquid heat on my chin, my lips, my jaw, and I fucking love being coated in her.

Nearly as much as I love the way her hands curl tighter through my hair, and she cries out, thrusting up into me, moaning, groaning, calling my name as she comes on my lips, then collapses.

I crawl up her body, brushing kisses on her skin as I go. I reach her face and she pulls me close, pressing her lips to mine. Without breaking the kiss, I grab the condom, open the wrapper, and then separate from her so I can roll it on. Can't fuck up this part. Got to do it properly.

I stare at her, all warm and glowing in my bed, her wild

blond hair fanned out, her eyes shimmering, and I'm floored. I'm here in my home with this wonderful woman I've completely fallen in love with.

And she's fallen right along with me.

How lucky am I?

She loops her arms around my neck. "Now," she begs.

"So demanding," I tease, as I rub the head of my dick against her wetness.

Holy hell. She feels amazing, and then I elevate that assessment to *divine* as I push into her. Her lips part, and she moans softly as I fill her. When I'm fully nestled inside her, she grabs the back of my head and brings my face close to hers.

"Hi," she whispers.

"Hey, you," I say as I start to move, stroking inside her, then dragging back, letting her feel the friction of us.

"You feel incredible," she says, and she never takes her eyes off me. She's so open, so vulnerable, so fucking honest.

A shiver runs down my spine as I take this all in. Our intense connection. The dark of the night. This woman in my bed. "Have I ever told you how much I love making you come?" I whisper as I thrust.

She flashes a quick smile. "No. Tell me," she murmurs.

I lower to my elbows, and she runs her fingernails up my arms and over my biceps, squeezing them.

I push deeper into her, savoring the wet heat, the snug

feel, the tightness of her as she grips me. "It's my new favorite hobby. Giving you orgasms," I say on a groan.

She digs her nails into my arms and arches up, her back bowing off the bed. "Oh God," she moans, her eyes falling shut. "You're so good at it."

"Because I love it. Because I love tasting you," I rasp in her ear. I circle my hips and drive into her. Her pitch rises as she moans. "Because I love making you feel good," I add, continuing my ode to her pleasure as I fuck her. She moves faster, matching me thrust for thrust, stroke for stroke. I meet her rhythm, then punch my hips, upping the pace, harder and faster. Her breath grows louder and wilder, and her legs wrap around me.

"Oh God," she groans.

I press my lips to her neck, then thread my hands in her hair, my chest to hers, our bare skin touching. "Because I'm so fucking in love with you," I say, and she rises up, grinding into me. Arching. Seeking.

Her mouth opens, and she's silent at first, then beautifully loud, as she shatters beneath me, writhing and moaning and breaking apart.

My own pleasure isn't far away. It's just within reach as I watch the climax move through her. Her breath catches. Her face contorts. Her pants turn to delirious cries.

That's all I need. She's all I want. I follow her to my own ecstasy, and it's never been better than it is with her.

CHAPTER TWENTY-TWO

Abby

Probably someone somewhere said no wise decisions were made at three in the morning. But I disagree.

As Simon wraps his arm around me, I ask, "So are we doing this?"

My heart beats faster, making a case for taking that leap. After all these months of fighting our feelings, I don't want to hide them anymore. I'm not blind. I'm not stupid. I know the risks. But this wild happiness in my heart when I'm with him? It's stronger than all those warning signs.

"Not sure how to break this to you, Abby," he deadpans, "but we've already done it. Twice in fact."

"You know what I mean!" I swat his chest. Have I mentioned he has a fantastic body? Just in case I haven't, I'll say it again. The man is cut, and strong, and muscled. His arms are shrine-worthy. His abs are lickable. And his ass deserves an award for firmness.

He runs his nose along my hair, inhaling me.

I shudder. "Don't distract me from talking."

"You're distracting me," he whispers.

Moonlight slices through the blinds in his room, casting a silvery glow across the covers. "I'm serious. Where do we go from here?"

He runs a hand gently through my hair. "Where do you want to go?"

"I don't know. I don't have an answer to how all this works. But I'm still in love with you." It scares me to voice the depth of my feelings, but they're real and true. My job matters, but so does my heart. With him, my heart is full.

This man brings me joy, and I don't just mean between the sheets. He makes me happy, and it's not because he fills a void in my life. It's not because I had a shitty childhood or a bad father—I had a good childhood and a great dad. And it's not because I have a history of ex-boyfriends who treated me like crap. I have none of that in my life story. I'm not damaged goods. I'm the twenty-something woman who loves her family and who loves her life.

Simon doesn't fill a void. He makes my life richer.

He nuzzles my neck. "Good. I'd have been devastated if you fell out of love with me after sex."

I can't help but smile. "Well, I didn't. Maybe I fell more in love."

He runs his hand along my ribs. "Same here," he whispers, his voice smoky and sexy. Then he clears his throat. I tense momentarily, but there's no need to worry when he says, "I want to figure this out. I want to be with you. I don't want you to lose your job. I know it might be weird if you work for my family if we're together like this, but it's not weird to me. I want you to be mine, Abby. Maybe I'm a greedy bastard, but can I have you in every way?" He grins, a sweet, lopsided grin.

I bring my index finger to my lips and adopt a pensive stare. "Hmm. So I can have the job and the guy? Sounds too good to be true."

"Maybe it's our time for all good things."

"And does that mean next time I ask you to play pool or go bowling with my friends and me, you'll go?"

He drops a quick kiss on my lips. "I will. But part of the reason I pulled away in the cab after our first kiss was that I didn't want to drag you down. Are you sure you don't care that I'm the guy with the kid?"

I roll my eyes. "Stop that. Stop saying that. Your daughter is not a deal-breaker. She's part of why I love you. And you could never drag me down."

He runs his hand along my arm. "Then we're doing this." He takes a beat. "Which also means I should tell Hayden." That's one of the biggest steps of all and my heart thumps harder as I wait for him to say more. "I'm not saying she needs to know everything, obviously. She's only five. But I want you in my life as more than her nanny, and that means I don't want to hide how I feel for you."

"I don't think I'm even capable of hiding how I feel anymore." Then, because I can, because we're stepping over the line that's no longer a line, I kiss him.

He's mine now.

He belongs to me.

* * *

Morning sun streaks through the window as lips flutter across my forehead. A soft voice whispers in my ear, "Going for a run. Back soon. Sleep more, my love."

"Running," I murmur with a shudder. "I choose sleeping." I slide back into blissful slumber.

When I wake up, I'm all alone. I stretch my arms over my head, savoring the new day and the chance to be with Simon—just us, all day long, being a couple. I peek at the clock. It's nearly nine. I make my way out of bed and head to his adjoining bathroom. It's all white with navy blue towels. Classy and masculine at the same time. The shower is huge by Manhattan standards, and I turn on the water, let it steam up, and then step under the shower-head. I use his body wash and his shampoo as I clean up, then turn off the water and wrap myself in a fluffy towel, with another for my hair.

I spot a toothbrush on the sink with a Post-It on it. *For you.* That brings a huge smile to my face, and after I brush my teeth, I towel-dry my hair, hang up one towel, and grab a hair-tie from my purse. I check my phone to find a text from him.

Simon: Leaving the park. Back in five minutes. I have good news!

I write back, and tell him *Can't wait*!

Then I drop my phone in my purse, wishing I had thought to bring a change of clothes, but *c'est la vie*. I'll head home shortly in last night's dress, after Simon returns. I'll change into something casual, and we'll spend the day together.

Or maybe I won't head home.

Maybe we'll spend the day naked in bed.

That possibility brings a wicked grin to my face.

It only widens when a knock on the door sounds through the apartment. I head to the living room, adjusting the towel over my breasts, spotting Simon's keys on the coffee table. He must have left them here, knowing I'd let him in when he returned from his run. Easier to run without keys, I guess.

I've never seen him return from a morning run before, and the image of him hot and sweaty from exercise kind of revs me up. Then again, everything about him turns me on. As I reach the door, I decide to let him know just how much. I drop my towel and turn the handle, yanking open the door.

My stomach craters.

My blood rushes cold, and my jaw drops when Miriam arches a haughty eyebrow. I slam the door as embarrassment floods every single corner of my body.

I run. I literally fucking sprint to Simon's room, yank open a drawer in his bureau, tug on a T-shirt of his.

But that's no better. I have nothing to wear on the bottom. Fuck a duck.

My heart bangs against my rib cage. The problem isn't just Miriam. It's the person with her. The little person. The one who matters. *My lover's daughter.*

I yank off his T-shirt, find my dress on the floor, pull it on, zip it up, and return to the entrance a minute later.

Then I take a deep breath, hold my chin up high, and open the door again.

"Abby!" Hayden calls out, but she doesn't rush into my arms like she usually does. Instead, she tilts her head to the side, a confused look on her face as she asks, "Why are you here on a Sunday morning? And why were you naked when you opened the door?"

I turn beet red, and the embarrassment multiplies. It digs roots. "I needed to take a shower," I stammer. At least there's some truth to that. "I didn't expect to see you two."

Miriam stares daggers at me. "That much is patently obvious," she says, then steps past me, bumping my shoulder as she strides into Simon's home.

"Where's Simon?"

"He's out for a run," I say.

"I texted to tell him I was bringing Hayden a day early."

Hayden parks her hands on her hips. "Do you open the door naked a lot?"

Cringing, I shake my head. "That was a mistake. I'm so sorry."

"It was weird," Hayden says. "But I'm still glad to see you. I'm just glad you have clothes on now."

Miriam runs her hand down Hayden's hair. "Don't get used to seeing her, darling. Gabby probably won't stick around."

"It's Abby," I correct.

Miriam sneers. "Abby. Gabby. Whatever it is. I'll be sure to let all my mommy friends know precisely how well you can be trusted around the fathers. Especially since I can't imagine you'll be here for much longer," she says in a low hiss.

The embarrassment morphs into something worse. Something that tastes like shame. This is not how I wanted Hayden to find out about her father and me—with me answering the door naked for her mother.

Five seconds later, there's another knock, and Hayden rushes to the door, yanking it open.

"I got the deal," he shouts happily at the same time his little girl cries out, "Daddy!"

His expression transforms in a second. Simon's eyes swing around his apartment from his daughter, to his ex-wife, to me.

This moment. This strangeness. This is exactly what I've dreaded, and it's not because of his ex. It's because I don't want to be the woman who sleeps with her boss.

Miriam breaks the awkward silence, and nails it.

"Well, well, well," she says to him. "Isn't this a bit of a cliché?"

CHAPTER TWENTY-THREE

Simon

I don't raise my voice, though I want to. But yelling at Miriam will get me nowhere. Even when she lashes out once more after Abby leaves and Hayden retreats to her room to play quietly.

Miriam pulls out a metal stool in the kitchen, parks herself on it, and shakes her head, as if she's a judge and she's oh-so disappointed in me. "Really, Simon? Banging the nanny?"

I burn inside. Clenching my fists, I will my tone to keep steady. "Pot. Kettle," I say quietly.

She laughs haughtily. "I did not sleep with the babysitter."

"You slept with your coworker," I say, then turn around, yank open the fridge, and grab the water pitcher. I pour a glass, reminding myself not to engage. This is what she's always loved. The battle. I down half the glass, then set it on the counter and turn to her again, calmer than I was a few seconds ago.

"But that's the past. And it doesn't matter," I say coolly, because I don't want to rehash what we hashed over and over at the time, and what led to our divorce when Hayden was two. What I want to know is why the fuck she's here a day early. "Does your phone not work? Why didn't you text me you were coming home a day early and bringing Hayden?"

"Don't you want your daughter with you as much as possible? Lord knows you fought me for that in the divorce."

I sneer. "You wanted that, too. You prefer it this way. Don't pretend this isn't what we both want."

She huffs. "I need to head to California tonight. I texted you this morning that I was bringing her by today."

"I didn't see a note from you."

"Well, I'm sure it's there. Go look."

I shake my head. "Doesn't matter."

"Why not? You seem to doubt me. Or do you not want to look through your text messages right now because there might be *naked* shots of the babysitter on your phone?"

My chest burns. I hate that I have to defend Abby right now. She did nothing wrong. "I'm not taking the bait, Miriam. I'm not even sure why you're here. You dropped off Hayden. You can say goodbye."

Miriam crosses her arms and stares down her nose at me. "I'm here because I'm beginning to question whether this arrangement works so well after all—now that I know you have naked trollops running around your home and answering the door in front of our soon-to-be kinder-gartener."

I breathe in through my nostrils, keeping all my anger inside. "One, she's not a trollop. Two, she's Hayden's nanny. Three, I'm allowed to be involved with whomever I choose to be involved with, and you and I both know there's no stipulation in any paperwork anywhere that says otherwise."

"But there could be," she says in a low hiss, the lobbyist viper in her rising to the surface. She knows how to fight, and that's what she's doing. That's the only reason to explain the intensity of her reaction. Then again, I wouldn't want to drop off Hayden at her home to be greeted by her naked beau. Even so, I won't let her turn this into something more.

I meet her cold stare. "Are you going to go there? You want to play dirty? We agreed when we split to do our best to keep it amicable for our daughter."

Miriam says nothing, just keeps her cool green gaze on me. I'm not going to let her win. I'm not going to roll over at this veiled attack that suggests I'm not fit to parent.

She's wrong.

She's dead wrong.

I might have fallen for the one person I'm not supposed to have, but it's only a line I shouldn't cross if Abby and I can't handle it. It's only forbidden if we keep letting ourselves believe we're doing something wrong. That together we're bad, or we've committed some sort of societal treason.

And, hell, maybe it is a cliché for a single dad to fall for the nanny. But fuck, it sure as hell isn't a crime. And it certainly isn't wrong.

If loving that amazing, vibrant, talented, brilliant woman is a cliché, then I'll gladly slap the sign on my chest. *I'm a cliché, and I'm okay with it.*

With that, I make a decision. To move on completely. To shed the fears that have held me back—ones about lines and boundaries, and who I should and shouldn't love. Loving Abby is the opposite of a mistake. It's *only* good. Because she makes me so goddamn happy.

"What are you grinning about?" Miriam asks.

I shrug it off. "I'm just happy," I say, speaking the plain truth. Even though I don't know where Abby is, or how she's feeling, or what Hayden thinks, I know I can work all that out. And even if Miriam makes veiled threats, I know they're full of hot air.

The more I let myself feel guilt and shame, the more those will dominate. But the sooner I embrace the utter fucking awesomeness of being *this* cliché, the happier I will be, and the better father I can be.

Abby makes me happy. Abby makes me better. Abby fulfills me in a way that only a good woman can. I've just got to make sure she knows we'll figure this out.

Miriam heaves a sigh. "Then can you see fit to let your sitter know to put some clothes on before she answers the door? Otherwise, next time I won't be so lenient about what's happening in front of young, impressionable eyes."

I straighten my shoulders and nod. Not because I agree, but because it's a helluva lot easier to let something go when you're bursting with a crazy kind of joy.

"Yes," I say, then see her to the door. "Goodbye, Miriam."

I turn around, and now it's time for me to sort out what to say to the two most important people in my life.

Starting with the littlest one.

CHAPTER TWENTY-FOUR

Abby

Harper's fiancé scrubs a hand over his jaw and shoots me a quizzical look.

"What is it, Nick?" Harper demands, smacking her palms on the table. "Speak. You obviously want to say something?"

He shakes his head, waves off Harper's question, and takes another drink of his iced chocolate here at Peace of Cake, where Harper and I were separated at birth. The cake I'm tunneling through is the size of my head. Don't judge. Who wouldn't devour cake after the ex-wife of the man she loved had seen her naked as a jaybird? The kid, too. Let's not forget the complete and utter embarrassment of my birthday suit parade.

I cringe as I swallow a bite of the German chocolate cake.

"You obviously have something on your mind," Harper says to Nick. "And considering you're the only guy at the table, you're going to need to spit it out and give us some insight into the mind of the man."

I called Harper as soon as I left the apartment, requesting an emergency meeting, and in the last ten minutes I've spilled all to them. This is too big a bowl of mortification to wallow in alone. I need company. Desperately.

"Say it. Tell us," I urge Nick.

"Honestly," he says, running a hand through his hair as he shrugs. "I just can't figure out why you didn't look through the peephole first?"

I squeeze my eyelids shut, but I don't escape the sound of Harper shushing him.

"What? It's a legit question," he says to her.

I open my eyes and answer. "Simon had just texted me that he'd be back in five minutes. Plus, he had left his keys behind. On top of that, Miriam wasn't supposed to bring Hayden home till tomorrow. It didn't even cross my mind that it would be her," I say with a sigh. "But the other thing is, I was excited. I wanted to do something kind of . . ."

"Naughty?" Harper supplies.

"Yes. Naughty. Dirty. Enticing. Not immensely stupid, which it obviously was, and clearly could have been avoided had I the simple good sense to check in the peephole." I toss my hands in the air. "But. . .IT DID NOT OCCUR TO ME."

Nick holds up his hands in surrender. "Question withdrawn."

I shoot him an apologetic smile. "Sorry. It's not you. I didn't mean to raise my voice. I just feel stupid. Like, put-a-webcam-on-me-and-watch-the-modern-female-in-the-city-do-completely-idiotic-things-in-the-name-of-new-love stupid."

Harper pats my hand and laughs lightly. "We all do stupid things when we're in love." She leans into Nick. "Right, babe?"

He nods. "Except me. I've never done anything stupid. I'm always completely cool and confident."

"Oh right," Harper says, nodding exaggeratedly. "Like the time you were jealous of Spencer's cat when he touched my boobs?"

I feign shock. "Harper, you let a pussycat feel you up?"

She wiggles her eyebrows. "I sure did." Then she drapes an arm around me. "Anyway, the point is, don't worry too much about it. Let's figure out what's next."

"You're right, but this whole morning was awful, the way Miriam looked at me and treated me. . ." I shudder, remembering how cruel and cold she was. "I can't believe that woman is Hayden's mother. Hayden is literally the best kid ever. I love that girl. I love her and adore her, and her mother is a witch."

Harper smirks like she has a secret up her sleeve.

"What?"

She glances at Nick then to me. "You love his kid."

"So? I nanny for her."

"You *love* his kid. You *love* him," Harper points out. "Whatever is going on, however the ex is behaving and however bad you feel, you'll sort it out because you love both of them. He's a package deal, and you're in love with the whole package."

"Package. She said package," Nick deadpans.

"You have such a dirty mind," I tell him.

He nods. "I can't help myself. I see innuendo. I walk right into it." Then he pushes his glasses higher. "But on a serious note, Abby, you like this guy. You like his kid. Who gives a fuck if his ex saw your boobs? Whatever. The kid will forget it, too. You just march right back there, and you take what's yours."

"Take what's mine," I say, repeating his pep talk, letting those words buoy me up. I straighten my shoulders and take a deep breath. I'm a fighter returning to the ring.

I'm taking what's mine.

With my chin up and my tough-girl attitude on, we move on from my woes and talk about Nick's new TV show, and how he and Harper are doing living together, and whether Nick will ever beat her at bowling.

But after I say goodbye to my friends and head through the Sunday morning throngs of New Yorkers grabbing their coffees, reading papers, taking selfies, and jogging on the streets, that certainty leaks away.

Taking what's mine is easier said than done. Because there's more at stake than pride.

I can get over a wound in my pride. I can move beyond a most awkward moment. This morning's incident will fade in the rearview mirror of our relationship as we move forward. But something bigger, heavier, weightier won't fade away.

Because how do I get over working for the man I love? Taking money from him?

Staying on as Hayden's nanny seemed fine at three in the morning, but that was the sex hormones leading me on, making me believe I could have my cake and eat it, too.

Now, as the sun rises higher, showing all the scratches and bruises of real life, I don't think it's all so blissfully easy.

Nor should it be.

The simple truth is this—I don't know how to work for him and love him. That seemed manageable before we smashed into each other. Before we fell hard and recklessly.

But the reality is that the moment in the foyer this morning underscores the central problem going forward.

I'll be getting a paycheck from the man who sees me naked.

CHAPTER TWENTY-FIVE

Simon

In Hayden's room, I sit on the floor with her and join her in a game of My Stuffed Elephant Can Fly. When she sets the elephant down, she shoots me a curious look. "Why was Abby naked?"

I keep the answer simple. No need to belabor it. "She was getting dressed, honey. She meant to answer the door in clothes. I know she's sorry."

Hayden shrugs. "Doesn't bother me. It was weird, though," she says, crinkling her nose.

I swipe a chunk of wild hair from her eyes, making sure she's meeting mine. "Are you going to be okay?"

She laughs. "Yes, Daddy. Want to play with me?"

And that's it. That's the joy of being five. She's no longer weirded out. But I also know the conversation isn't over. The part that matters hasn't even begun.

"Hey, sweet pea," I say, as I grab a stuffed giraffe to join her in whatever game we're playing.

She looks at me, her big, hazel eyes innocent, waiting.

"What would you think if I told you I liked Abby?"

She lights up, a big grin spreading across her face. "I like her, too!"

"What if it was more than like? What if I loved her? You know, how a man and a woman love each other?"

Her jaw drops, and her eyes sparkle. "I love Abby! And you love Abby!"

She makes the elephant fly right into her toy chest, where she grabs her wooden play sword. "Does that mean you can both take me fencing again? Because I loved it and I want to keep doing it."

I smile and grab her waist, bringing her in for a hug, wooden sword and all. This part is simple. Loving my girl. "I hope so, sweet pea. I'd really like that."

"What about tonight?"

"I don't think there are any fencing classes tonight."

"Then tomorrow?"

"I'll see."

"Can Abby go, too, since you like her now?"

"I hope she can."

I plant a kiss on Hayden's forehead, then proceed to make the giraffe battle the elephant until we both crack up and flop onto her purple carpet, laughing.

Some things in life are easy.

* * *

Someone raps on the door softly after nine. Expecting Abby, I rise from the couch, my heart beating overtime as

I cross the distance to the green door to unlock it. Today didn't go as planned at all, but I can't wait to tell her how easily the talk with Hayden went.

When I turn the handle, the sight of her knocks the breath from my chest. She wears white jeans, the kind that land at her calves, and a bright, pretty pink tank top with a shiny metal pattern around the neck. A dangly silver pendant falls against her chest.

My thoughts immediately leap to how that necklace would look between the creamy flesh of her breasts while she wears nothing else.

"Hayden's asleep," I tell her, so she knows the score.

She nods as she walks inside and drops a quick kiss on my cheek. "Tell me all about the deal. I'm dying to know."

I love that she asks, that she's excited about this business opportunity.

I let the door fall behind her, take her hand, and bring her to the couch. When I sit next to her, our knees touch. "He wants to be in business together. That means I'm the lucky son of a bitch who gets to give him money," I say, then laugh at that statement. "Gabriel truly is in the driver's seat."

"He is amazingly talented. It's a wise choice, Simon. For both of you. You guys just *get* each other. You're the business smarts that he needs to balance his artistic soul."

I smile at the compliment. "Thank you. Not gonna lie —I'm pretty damn excited. This is exactly the sort of deal

I've wanted to make. He's got all these plans for growing the business. He has vision, and I think he can become a true rock-star chef."

"And you get to be a part of that," she says, pride in her voice, admiration in her eyes. The support she shows warms my bones. I'm so damn lucky to have a chance with a woman like her.

"You predicted it," I say, reminding her of what she'd said after the dinner with him in the Village.

She shrugs as if it's no big deal. "I had a good feeling, but I also believed in you."

"But you know it wouldn't have happened without you, Abby." Keeping my eyes on hers, I squeeze her fingers. "You played a huge part, teaching me the right phrases, helping me to converse with them. You were a key part of this."

I brush my lips to her temple, her cheek, her mouth. She parts her lips, and my heart thumps hard against my chest. I kiss her, slow and tender, savoring every second of her touch. Her kiss is everything good in the world.

"I'm sorry for all the trouble earlier," she says when we break the kiss. "When I opened the door for Miriam."

Shaking my head, I press my finger to her lips. "Don't apologize, beautiful. You have nothing to be sorry for."

She lightly pushes my hand away. "I want to say this," she says, her voice strong, reminding me that she's no pushover. "I need you to understand why I did it. I wanted to surprise you naked. I had this image of you opening the door, seeing me with nothing on, and feeling I was your gift."

My skin heats up all over, and a million naughty thoughts fight their way to the front of my brain. "You are a gift," I say softly, reaching for her, threading my hand through her blond curls. She sighs sexily as I touch her, and that small sound is such a relief. Maybe there was a part of me that was worried that she'd be scared away. But Abby's not like that. She's tough. She's strong. And she has a heart that's willing to let me in, baggage and all.

She presses her palms to my chest, giving a light push. Her eyes are intense. "That's what I want to be to you. A gift."

"You are. You absolutely are." I tilt my head, studying her face. I inch back. "Why do I feel like there's a 'but' in that statement?"

She takes a breath and lets it out. "Because. There is."

My heart craters. Shit. After last night, after today, after all these months—I don't want to lose her. "What is it?" I ask, dread in my tone.

She doesn't let go of me, though. Her hands travel up my chest to my shoulders, then into my hair. Ah, that's better. Fuck dread. Whatever is coming, we can handle it, as long as her hands are on me.

"Here's the thing . . . I love you, and I love your daughter, but I don't think I can work for you anymore."

I frown. Her words barely compute. "Why? I thought we talked about this last night? That we were going to find a way for this all to work."

She raises her chin. "We did talk about it. At night. After amazing sex," she says, playing with the ends of my hair. "When we were all dopey and happy."

"The sex will be amazing again, so just be prepared for more of that."

She runs her fingers down my neck, making me shudder. "I know. I know it'll be incredible."

"Jesus Christ, you're driving me crazy with every little touch." My voice is practically a growl.

"That's my point," she says, as her fingers travel over my shoulders and down my arms. "I want to touch you like this. But Simon, I don't feel right being your lover and your employee. It's not what I want for myself."

"But," I say, stumbling on words. My muscles tense, and worry thrums through me even as she draws lazy circles on my biceps. "What do you want?"

She tilts her head like a curious cat. "Don't you get it?"

"No. Spell it out."

"I want to be with you, silly. I want to run my hands in your hair and down your arms. I love you, and I want to go to dinner with you, and the movies, and send naughty text messages, and take showers together and learn exactly how top-notch the rating is when it's you and me in the shower." Her words thrill me and turn me on. Then she melts me when she says, "And I love your daughter."

She takes a beat then adds, "But I can't be your employee, and you can't pay me if you want to make love to me. So if you want me in your life, this is how you can have me. I'll be yours, and I'll be with you as your girlfriend, and with Hayden as her father's girlfriend. But I can't work for you."

And hell if I don't fall deeper into love with her this second. My heart leaps out of my chest into her hands. She is so goddamn giving, so loving. I press a kiss to her forehead. "You're the most incredible woman I've ever known, but I can't let you do that."

"But you can't stop me, either."

"I know. That's the issue. I can't stop you from quitting. But this feels unfair. Unfair to you." This bothers me immensely. There has always been an imbalance of power between us. I've been her boss. She's been my employee. But now, if she's cutting that thread to make the sacrifice for *us* as a couple, the power tips even more unfairly in my direction.

She's losing her job. *For me.* "This is crazy. I don't want you to be without work. I have enough money. I've made plenty already. You shouldn't be the one to lose her job."

"It's okay. I'll find another one soon enough, and I'll stay until you find someone else. I'm not going to leave you in the lurch with Hayden. But I can't be the person I want to be if I work for you and sleep with you and spend my nights with you. And I want to do things together with you and your girl, as a couple."

I cup her cheeks, getting lost in those beautiful eyes. "I want to do all those things with you. But I don't want you to be the one who gives up a job. I want to take care of you."

She smiles but shakes her head. "I can take care of myself."

"I know you can. Your fierceness and your independence are what I love about you. But you've got to see that I want to help."

I can't let Abby bear all the burden. But I don't know how to fix this, either, and that drives me crazy. For a few seconds I toss around a number of alternatives in my head, then like ten tons of obvious falling from the sky, the answer is crystal clear. I know what I need to do, and how to fix this for her. "I'm not the kind of man who's going to let the woman he loves take the leap alone."

"Okay," she says slowly. "And that means what?"

"Do you trust me?"

She nods.

"I know how to make deals. And I have one in mind. Give me a bit to work this out."

She fiddles with the rolled-up cuffs of my shirt. "I can't wait to hear what you have up your sleeve." Then she plays with the collar. "But I'll say this. I do think it's going to be really weird for you to have another nanny."

I laugh.

She's right on that account. But not if I hire the right one.

CHAPTER TWENTY-SIX

Abby

A new student enters my Spanish class the next morning.

I do a double take then nod a silent hello. His face is familiar, and so is his smile.

He answers the questions I pose during class. He answers them perfectly.

Because he's fluent.

At the end of the lesson when my other students leave, Gabriel strides up to me and extends his hand. "So good to see you again, Abby."

"And you, as well, Gabriel," I say as I gather up my class notes and materials. "But I didn't think you needed a class."

He shrugs impishly. "I don't."

"Exactly," I say with a grin. "So what brings you here?"

He strokes his chin. "My new investor had an idea that I think might be rather brilliant."

I arch an eyebrow as I slide my purse strap up my shoulder. "Your new investor is rather bright."

"He is. And he reminded me that all these expansion plans are well and good . . . but that I might need some training for my employees."

"And what sort of training would that be?"

"I will need someone who is good at teaching," he says, sweeping his arm toward the now-empty classroom. "Someone who can help all my current and future employees attain fluency in the languages required to do business in my multi-national company and my restaurants around the world."

My smile spreads, widening across my face. I had a feeling that was what Simon was up to—using his deal-making skills to make something magical happen for me. Something on my own terms.

"That's why I came here today. To see if you're as good with teaching as I suspected."

"And your conclusion?"

"You're even better," he says, then takes a beat. "I know you hold classes and tutor, but I would love to offer you contract work teaching languages at my company, if you're able to fit it into your schedule."

His excitement is infectious. His offer is enticing. It's exactly the type of work I love. "It seems I have more time than I did recently, so I'd love to hear more about what you have in mind."

I leave the classroom with Gabriel, and we head out for coffee and to talk more about his plans. I'll certainly miss taking care of Hayden all day, but she's starting kindergarten in a few months, and this seems like the perfect next job for me. Simon might have played a role as the matchmaker, but I don't doubt my skills and talent are what seal the deal.

And that's how I like to roll.

Besides, I'll be seeing plenty more of Hayden and Simon, and in a whole new way.

* * *

Simon

A few days later, Harper nabs a spare, thrusts her arms in the air, then high-fives Abby.

Nick drops his forehead in his palm and shakes his head. "Damn. I will never beat her."

He raises his face and shrugs as the guy next to us launches an emerald green ball that rips down the lane.

"She's just too good," I say. We're at the bowling alley that Harper and Nick love, and Abby stole me away from work for an early evening game of guys versus girls. Hayden is with Madison at one of those do-it-yourself pottery places.

"I swear Harper was a bowling pro in a past life."

"And I'm convinced I played centerfield for the Yankees in another life," I say, and Nick laughs.

I steal a glance at my watch.

Nick taps the screen where he's keeping score. "You gotta go? Or think you can nail a strike with that once-was-an-outfielder arm to win for us?"

I grin. "I'll do my best."

I grab the bowling ball and send it rolling along the hard wood in a smooth line, knocking down all ten pins. Nick pumps a fist. "Dude, I need you on my team, like, forever."

I blow on my fingers, too hot to handle. "And on that note, I need to pick up Hayden."

Abby walks over and wraps her hand around my arm. "Thanks for joining us."

Nick scratches his chin and seems deep in thought for a moment. "Hey man, if you ever need someone to watch your kid so you guys can go out, Harper and I would be happy to help."

Harper nods enthusiastically, and Abby smiles as wide as I've ever seen. As for me? Well, the offer is a shot of sunshine straight in the heart. There once was a time when I figured I wouldn't fit in with her friends—that I'd be the odd man out.

Instead, the opposite has happened. So, I accept his offer for Friday night. By then, I should have everything in place to tell Abby my plan.

* * *

Tyler raises his beer glass. "You're really going to do it?"

I nod and repeat, "I'm really going to do it."

He tips his glass to mine and clinks. We're at Speakeasy, a swank bar in midtown that his cousin's wife runs. "I'm proud of you."

"Thank you. A man's got to do what a man's got to do."

Tyler downs a gulp of his pale ale as music plays from the speakers above us. "Damn straight. And this might be the ballsiest, coolest move you've ever made, Travers."

I beam, pride bursting in my chest. "I think so, too." I take a thirsty drink of my beer then set down the glass. "And by the way, your plan to win back Delaney is one hundred percent certified insane."

Tyler laughs and nods as a pair of women in slouchy tops and skinny jeans walk past us, one of them checking out my friend. He wiggles his eyebrows in their direction. "It is insane. Especially since I could, you know, start over with someone new."

"You could, but that's not what you want."

He shakes his head with a sigh. "Not at all. I'm getting her back."

"I won't bet against you, even though I've got a hundred-dollar bill that says you won't make it through the front door."

He offers his hand to shake. "Oh, ye of little faith. You're on."

After we seal the bet, I down more of the beer then point to our drinks. "In case you're wondering, I did use the hundred I won from you for these brews."

He crinkles his nose. "Dude, this is my cousin's wife's bar. I'm going to lose my lunch, knowing where that's been."

"I deposited it, dickhead. That was a credit card I used for these."

"Then you infected some poor bank employee," he says, shaking his head as if he's disappointed with me.

"I'm the worst. Simply the worst."

"You're the worst," he agrees. Then he takes a deep breath and nods a few times, as if he's thinking about something. "Your plan is epic, man."

And in a few hours, after Abby finishes her day with Hayden, I'll take her out and tell her.

"Thank you. And yours might very well prove to be epic, too."

He raises a glass one more time. "To our epic selves."

"And to the women who'll have us."

"Bless those angels," Tyler adds.

Angels, indeed. That's a perfect way to describe my Abby.

CHAPTER TWENTY-SEVEN

Abby

That night, Harper pretends to make a pencil go through her nose and come out her ear. Hayden's eyes widen, and she claps several times.

"Again! Again! Do it again, and teach me, please!"

Nick laughs from his spot on the couch. "She never reveals the secrets of her tricks."

Harper waggles her hands in a now-you-see-it-now-you-don't style. "He's right. But I'll gladly do it again."

As my magician friend shows off more sleight-of-hand, I grab my purse from the coffee table. Meanwhile, Nick draws a cartoon of a pirate, as per Hayden's request. The magician and the cartoonist—I can't think of better jobs for a pair of babysitting friends to have.

"Now, don't let her trick you into thinking she can stay up late," Simon tells Harper as he wraps an arm around his daughter's little shoulder. "This little lady has an eight o'clock bedtime."

Harper winks at Hayden, then nods solemnly at Simon. "I'd never do that. We'll make sure she goes to bed on time, and we'll make doubly sure that she doesn't eat any of the mint chocolate-chip ice cream that we didn't bring."

"We have ice cream? You didn't tell me that," Nick says, playing along with Harper.

"What about Skittles?" Hayden asks. "I love Skittles, too."

Harper waves a hand behind Hayden's ear and produces a mini bag of Skittles. Hayden claps, and Simon shrugs happily. "Have all the sugar you want," he says to his girl, then to Harper and Nick, "And you guys have fun when she's bouncing off the walls."

"We absolutely will," Harper says.

I was blown away when Nick had offered to babysit at the bowling alley. Harper had seconded him and later told me, "I don't want your relationship with His Hotness to be dependent on when his ex-wife has the kid. If you want to have a date during the week, you can count on us to help out with Hayden."

It was simply an offer we couldn't refuse. Simon's sister Kristy has offered to babysit for us, too, and I'm sure we'll lean on her some night soon.

Simon says thank you to Harper and Nick, and I love that he's getting to know my friends better and hanging out with them, too. I want him to be a part of my "family" here in New York.

We leave and walk in the warm summer night to a new fusion-cuisine restaurant off Park Avenue, which Eduardo has been raving about.

After the meal, Simon raises a glass of wine and toasts to me then to us.

He clears his throat. "There's something I want to tell you. It's not bad, I swear," he adds, with that smile I adore.

I run the toe of my black high heel along his leg under the table. "Better not be bad."

"So," he says, setting down his wine and clasping his hands together. "I found a new nanny."

My eyes widen. "Already? You didn't even let the body get cold."

"Hey, now! You left me."

"Who did you find? And how on earth did you pull that off so quickly? This is New York City. It's not easy finding a good nanny, especially to replace, like, the best nanny ever," I say, pointing at myself.

"That's true. You're a tough act to follow."

"So, who is she?"

He takes a drink of his wine.

I park my chin in my hand and stare at him. "Waiting."

He points a thumb at himself.

I frown in confusion.

"You're looking at him," he says.

My jaw drops. "What?"

Reaching across the table for my hand, he continues, "Remember when I said I used to work too much?"

I nod, flashing back to our conversation at the French café the day of our first kiss. "I do."

His voice turns soft and vulnerable as he laces his fingers through mine. "I don't want to become that guy again. And I feel like I have a new chance with you, Abby. To do things differently. To be a better man."

A lump rises in my throat. "You're already an amazing man. You don't have to change for me."

He clasps my hand tighter. "Thank you. But I want to change some things. I want to make sure I can be that man for you and for my daughter. If I drive myself into the ground working too much, that's no good for anyone. I want to be around for both of you."

"So you're not hiring anyone? You're going to do it all yourself?" I tilt my head to the side. "I don't get it. That's even harder, since you have all this work now with Gabriel's venture. It seems like you'd be even busier."

"I would . . . if I were an active investor," he says. "But I talked to Gabriel a few days ago and said I'd rather front the money and then take a backseat role. I told him I'd prefer not to be involved as much in the day-to-day, and he said he could deal with those terms. I'll make sure he has all the right people in place to execute his plans, and then I can step back. Besides, he already has talented people working for him. Present company included," he says, tipping his head to me.

"And he was fine with that?"

Simon smiles and nods. "Incredibly fine with it. Plus, Hayden will be starting kindergarten in the fall, so I'll have a few hours each day while she's in school to work on Gabriel's business or on whatever new opportunity comes my way. I'll still benefit from what I expect will be his success, he'll still benefit from my investment, and in exchange I gain something invaluable," he says, his blue eyes holding my gaze. "*Time.*"

A tear slips down my cheek. I'm happy for him. For the choices he's making. For the way he wants to live his life and raise his daughter. "I love that," I say softly.

"Time is the most precious thing of all, and the easiest resource to waste if we aren't careful. I'm lucky because I already have more than enough money to pay the bills. Now, with this choice, I can have time to spend with my two favorite people in the world—you and Hayden. I don't need to hire someone to replace you, because I want to be there for my girl."

How can I not fall more in love with him for this choice? The fact that he's such a great dad has always been part of the allure for me. It's been massively appealing how good he is with his daughter. What can I say? I thought I was an everything girl, but it turns out one of the things I like most in a man is how good he is at taking care of his kid. That's my penchant. Some women go for arms, some like humor, and some love a bad boy.

Me? I'm drawn to this amazing, gorgeous, handsome single father. I want to smother him in kisses and then jump his bones. "You know it's ridiculously hot how much you love your kid?"

He grins broadly. "You're just ridiculously hot."

"I mean it," I say seriously. "You have to know that's one of the reasons I fell in love with you." I place my hand on my heart. I can feel it flutter. "The way you are with Hayden *melts* me."

A slow smile spreads on his face, and he whispers, "Thank you."

"And I can't think of anyone more perfect for the job," I add.

"Yours are big shoes to fill, though."

I wag a finger at him. "Hey, handsome. Don't think you're ever wearing my shoes."

He cracks up, holding his hands in surrender. "I don't want to wear your shoes. But I wouldn't mind taking yours off and undressing you."

I survey the restaurant. "At this fine dining establishment?" I ask in mock surprise.

He shakes his head. "Let's get out of here, beautiful."

He pays the check and takes my hand, threading his fingers through mine. His touch is possessive, his firm grip reminding me how strong he is, and that strength turns me on.

Outside, he quickly hails a cab, and on the drive to my tiny apartment, we kiss like crazy. His hands loop through my hair, and his lips claim mine. Then he travels to my neck, and my body hums with desire for him.

Soon, but hardly soon enough, the cab arrives at my building. The instant the door to my apartment shuts, his hands are all over me. We frantically tear at buttons and zippers, undressing and stumbling to my couch. Shoes come off, socks, pants, my skirt, my top, and his shirt. My hands explore his chest, his firm muscles, and those arms I can't get enough of.

"We only have thirty minutes. The sitters need to go home," I tease.

He wiggles his eyebrows. "So much I can do to you in thirty minutes," he says, as he strips off my bra and panties. We sink onto the couch, naked together, then he kisses me like he can't get enough of me while his fingers glide between my legs. I moan and sigh and murmur.

I'm in heaven with him. The way he touches me is everything I've ever fantasized about. I want to give my body to him, let him have me, take me, because he knows just what to do. I lift my hips as he strokes me, his mouth on my neck, my shoulder, my breasts.

As my sounds grow louder, he groans hungrily, pressing his firm body to mine, his erection hot and heavy against my skin. His arousal turns me molten, and it's not long before I'm shattering in his hand, calling his name.

As I come down from my orgasm, I grab his shoulders and pull him on top of me, opening my legs for him. "I want you. I need you. I've missed you," I tell him, because it's been a few nights since we've been intimate. I've learned quickly that dating a single father means *alone time* is hard to come by. I'm not going to say that's ideal. But I'll say this—it makes me want him more.

Right now, I ache for him. Exquisitely.

"Missed you, too," he says, as he clasps my wrists, pins them over my head, and rubs his erection against my center. I moan loudly and arch into him.

"Condom," he mutters. "Let me grab one."

I wrap my legs around his bare ass, not letting him go. I shake my head. "I'm on the pill. Are you safe?"

He nods. "So safe," he says, and that's all I need to know.

He sinks into me, and I'm in another world with him. Sheer, unadulterated pleasure spreads through my body as he makes love to me. He pins my arms above my head the whole time, and I love how he overpowers me, how he takes me, how he moves inside me, whispering sweet nothings.

Love you. Need you. Crazy for you.

Then the tempo shifts, and so do his words.

Fuck. So hot. So tight. I want you to come all over me.

He thrusts faster, harder, deeper, and now this is fucking, pure, carnal fucking, as the man I love is wild with me, exactly how I want him right now. He takes me to the edge, as all the white-hot pleasure in my body curls inward then bursts into a thousand fiery sparks.

In seconds, he follows me there, groaning my name as he comes inside me.

He breathes out hard, and I sigh happily. So damn happily. I wrap my arms tighter around him, savoring the afterglow.

Our chests are sweat-slicked, but I don't want to separate from him. Instead, I lace my fingers in his hair. I kiss his cheek, his eyelids, his lips. "Did you know I'm dating the hottest manny in New York?"

He cracks up, and I laugh, too. He's so much more than a manny. So much more than the hot single dad.

He's the best man I know.

EPILOGUE

Simon

Three months later

Hayden swings our hands together as we head down the tree-lined block in the east 80s, on the way to her first day of kindergarten. She skips, and to say she's eager to start school is an understatement. My girl is fearless, and it's one of the things I most admire about her.

"And if the teacher asks how you spent your summer, what will you say?" I ask.

"So much stuff! I learned how to fence, and I became awesome at it," she declares, and that's sort of true. Surprisingly, she's stayed with the sport, attending lessons and classes a few days a week. Taking her to the club is one of my favorite things to do, partly because she enjoys it so much, and partly because Abby joins us at nearly every class and we watch her progress together. Abby cheers her on and gives her tips, and then we lean closer, talking about how great she's doing. I'm sure if anyone paid attention to us, they'd gag over how adorably in love we are.

Let them.

Fucking let them.

"That's true," I say. "You're a regular pirate musketeer sword fighter. What else?"

"We went to London and saw the big jewels," she continues, and that trip was fantastic, too. The three of us rode the London Eye, visited Big Ben, checked out the museums, and admired the crown jewels.

"And we were all perfectly fluent in the language," I tease.

"Except they talk funny over there. But funny good," she says as we near the school entrance. "Oh wait! There was one more thing that happened this summer. The baby eagles left their nest. We watched the eaglets become eagles."

"We sure did," I say, and that was yet another thing the three of us did together. Funny, how the eaglets in the poplar tree became matchmakers for Abby and me. Checking out "Eagle TV" every day, trading texts—experiencing little moments of those hatchlings growing into badass birds of prey—played a part in the two of us falling in love.

Eagles and zebras, French braids and restaurants, angel food cake and language lessons, and so many stolen moments that turned real.

At the school, I give my daughter a big hug goodbye, then I wave as she heads through the doors. As I walk away, I check the time.

Abby's at work and won't be free until lunch, so I duck into a coffee shop and use my phone to catch up on a few small business items that need my attention. As I enjoy a coffee, I answer an email about a new project I'm dabbling in—dabbling is the way I like to work these days. A few hours while Hayden's in school is all I need to satisfy the business itch.

When I wrap up the email, I call it a day. I wander up Lexington for an hour, then back down, enjoying the September morning that rolls into noon, when I meet the woman of my dreams for lunch at a sidewalk café on Seventy-Eighth Street, with a chalkboard menu out front.

She greets me with a kiss, soft and delicious, which leaves me wanting more. Somehow, I manage not to turn it R-rated.

"You look gorgeous," I tell her.

"As do you. So give me all the details," she says as she sits down. "How was the drop-off? Was she nervous? Or fearless?"

"Guess."

"Fearless, of course," she says, beaming.

I tell her everything, and then we talk about her morning teaching and her lesson plans for the rest of the week. When the meal ends, I walk her back to work, giving her another kiss that I hope leaves her longing for kisses later tonight that don't stop.

"Can't wait till bedtime," I whisper.

"Me, too."

That's because we live together now.

We're not the Brady Bunch family. Sometimes we argue. Sometimes we're tired. But you know what? Somehow, it's all working out, and I'm the happiest guy in the world with the two ladies in my life—the girl I love madly and the woman I adore to the ends of the earth.

They are my everything.

ANOTHER EPILOGUE

Simon

A little later . . .

Lights twinkle on the dance floor as I take the woman in black into my arms.

"This dress is gorgeous," I tell her, my eyes raking over Abby's basic black sheath. She wears heels that look to be four inches, and she's still little, like she told me she would be. But we fit perfectly as she glides against me, swaying to the music at Harper and Nick's wedding. "But it has nothing on you. You look amazing, my love."

"Thank you. It hardly looks like a bridesmaid's dress," she says, glancing up at me as she runs her fingers down my tie. "And you are as handsome as ever."

"Thank you. And your friends are so happy." I nod in the direction of the bride and groom enjoying a slow dance.

"They're your friends now, too," Abby points out.

I nod. "You're right. They are."

I love how our lives have meshed. We've had dinner and evenings out with Kristy and Tyler, and the two of us have played pool with her gang of friends, too. She's no pool shark, though. She still can barely knock in a ball. Seems every time I try to teach her, we get distracted.

No complaints there.

No complaints anywhere.

In fact, as my eyes scan the reception room, I can only think of one thing that would make my life better. *This.*

Maybe it's too soon. It's definitely unplanned. But the second the idea touches down, it takes hold and digs roots. And I know, beyond a shadow of a doubt, that it needs to be our next step.

I cup her cheek in my hand. "Marry me."

She startles and wrenches back. "What?"

"I love you madly. I want to be with you always. We should get married."

She blinks, parts her lips, and speaks slowly, each word taking its time. "Are you really proposing to me right now?"

I laugh, mostly at myself. "Yeah. I am." Then I brush a kiss to her lips. "I didn't plan this. I don't have a ring. But I'll take you shopping tomorrow. All I know is I want to spend the rest of my life with you. I want *this*," I say, casting my gaze around the room, "for us. Forever."

I hold her face in my hands and look into her eyes. They're shiny, and she licks her lips. And then, I propose. "I love you. God, how I love you. I want to marry you. Will you marry me?"

* * *

Abby

I'm not a girl who dreamed of a man getting down on one knee in a horse-drawn carriage. I've never expected a shiny ring presented in a champagne glass.

All I've ever hoped for is this kind of love.

I have it, and I have so much more.

And that's why his unexpected and unplanned proposal is perfect for us. It comes from his heart, and that's how I answer him—from mine.

There is only one answer.

"Yes."

THE END

Did you enjoy getting to know Simon's buddy Tyler? Stay tuned for THE HOT ONE, Tyler and Delaney's second-chance love story, releasing in March 2017! But first, get ready for things to heat up for Gabriel and his love interest, Penny, the woman who runs the Little Friends dog shelter, where Wyatt (WELL HUNG) and Nick (MISTER O) volunteer. THE ONLY ONE releases in December!

THE ONLY ONE

Let's say there was this guy. And he gave you the most mind-blowing night of sex in your life. And you never saw him again.

Until ten years later.

Now, it turns out he's the ONLY ONE in all of Manhattan whose restaurant is available the night of my charity's big event.

The trouble is, he doesn't recognize me.

* * *

This woman I'm working with is so damn alluring. The first time I set eyes on her, I was captivated, and I can't get her out of my mind. Even if it's risky to tango with someone I'm working with, she's a risk I'm willing to take.

The trouble is, she won't give me the time of day.

But I'm determined to change that.

THE HOT ONE

At first glance, stripping naked at my ex-girlfriend's place of work might not seem like the brightest way to win her back. But trust me on this—she always liked me best without any clothes on. And sometimes you've got to play to your strengths when you're fighting an uphill battle. I'm prepared to fight for her . . . and to fight hard.

* * *

The goddamn nerve of Tyler Nichols to reappear in my life like that, all sculpted muscle, toned abs, and a hard body that drove me wild far too many nights. Not to mention the knowing grin, those mischievous eyes, that chestnut hair I want to run my fingers through. That man is nothing but a cocky, arrogant jerk. A cocky jerk. A jer . . .

Except . . . he's not any of those things at all.

That's what makes it so tough to resist the HOT ONE . . .

COMING SOON!
THE ONLY ONE

PROLOGUE

Penny

Ten years ago

The clock mocks me.

As the minute hand ticks closer to eight in the evening, I wrack my brain to figure out if I got the time wrong. Maybe we picked two. Maybe he said ten. Maybe we're meeting tomorrow. My chest twists with a desperate anxiety as I toy with the band on my watch.

But as the fountains of Lincoln Center dance higher under the waning light, I'm sadly certain there was no error in communication.

The only error was one of judgment.

Mine.

Thinking he'd show.

Drawing a deep, frustrated breath, I peer at my watch once more, then raise my face, searching the crowds that wander past the circular aquatic display at Manhattan's epicenter for the performing arts. This fountain is so romantic; that's why we chose it as the place to meet again.

One week later.

Foolishly I hunt for the amber eyes and dark wavy hair, for the lean, tall frame, for that mischievous grin that melts me every time.

I listen for the sound of him amidst the melody of voices, wishing to hear his rise above the others, calling my name, apologizing in that sexy accent of his for being late.

My God, Gabriel's accent was a recipe for making a young woman weak in the knees. That was what he had done to me. The man melted me when I first met him last month in Barcelona at the tail end of my summer of travels across Europe.

When I close my eyes and float back in time, I hear that delicious voice, just a hint of gravel in his tone, and a whole fleet of butterflies chase each other in my belly at the resurgence of that faraway romantic dream.

I open my eyes, trying to blink away the inconvenient intrusion of memory. I should go. It's clear he's not coming tonight.

But, just in case I mixed up the times, maybe I'll give him one more minute. One more look. One more scan of the crowd.

I let the clock tick past eight.

I still don't see him.

I've been here for more than two hours, sitting on the black marble edge of the fountain. Scouring the corners of Lincoln Center. Peering left, then right down Columbus. Circling, like an animal at a zoo—*pathetic modern-day female waiting for male to stay true to his word.*

Sure, one hundred twenty-plus minutes is not much time in the grand scheme of life, but when the person you're waiting for doesn't show, it's a painful eternity of disillusionment.

I wish we had picked midnight to meet because then I'd have an excuse for him. I'd wonder if midnight meant yesterday or perhaps today. But "six in the evening, on the first of the month, as dusk casts its romantic glow over Manhattan"—his words—is perfectly clear.

He was supposed to be on his way to New York for a job. I'd already landed a plum assignment in this city. Fate appeared to have been looking out for us, and so we'd made plans. One week ago, we'd drunk sangria and danced on the sidewalks of Barcelona, to street musicians playing the kind of music that made you want to get close to someone, and he'd cupped my cheek, saying, "I will count down the days, the hours, the minutes until six in the evening on the first day of September."

Then he'd taken me to his room, wearing that dark and dirty look in his hazel eyes. A look that told me how much he wanted me. Words had fallen from his lips over and over that last night in Spain as he'd undressed me, kissed me all over, and sent me soaring. *My Penelope, give me your body. Let me show you pleasure like you've only imagined.*

Cocky bastard.

But he was right. He'd made all my fantasies real.

He'd made love to me with such passion and sensuality that my traitorous body can still remember the imprint of his hands on my skin, the caress of his delicious lips leaving sizzling marks everywhere.

Standing, I run a hand down my pretty red sundress with the tiny white dots and the scoop neck. He loved me in red. One night we'd walked past a boutique that sold dresses like this. He'd wrapped his arms around me from behind and planted soft, sultry kisses on the back of my neck. "You'd look so lovely in that, my Penelope. And even lovelier when I take it off you. Actually, just wear nothing with me."

I'd shuddered then.

I hurt now as the memory snaps cruelly before my eyes.

I turn away from the fountain, swiping a hand across my cheek. The seed of discouragement planted in the first minutes after he failed to appear has sprouted over the two hours I've waited for him. It's twisted into a thorny weed of disappointment that's lodged deep in my chest.

There are no two ways about it. My three-day love affair under the starry Spanish sky with the man who whispered sweet nothings in my ear while he played my body like a virtuoso pianist isn't getting a second act.

Gabriel has my email.

He knows how to reach me.

He chose not to.

Que sera, sera.

I refuse to cry.

With my chin held high, I walk away.

The rest of the night, the hurt deepens, burrowing into my bones.

The next day, shame wraps itself around that weed in my chest, dominating my emotions. Shame for having believed him. For having bought the damn dress. For having hope.

When I open my closet, I swear the red dress laughs at me. I huff, yank it off the hanger, and stuff it in a grocery bag. I grab the pink one I wore the day I met him, then the soft yellow skirt I had on the next day we were together, which made for such easy access. When I pull down the silky blue tank next, I'm walloped with a reminder of his reaction when he first saw me in it.

His eyes had widened, and he'd groaned appreciatively. "Beautiful."

It was all he'd said, then he'd kissed the hollow of my throat and blazed a sensual trail up my neck, along my jawline to my ear, and whispered, "So beautiful in blue."

I'd melted.

I'd believed all his sweet, swoony words. He'd said so many things that had set my skin on fire, that had made my heart hammer, that had made my panties damp.

Even now, as I clutch the clothes I wore with him, then didn't wear with him, goosebumps rise on my flesh. I squeeze my eyes shut and tell myself to burn the house down.

It's the only way.

I leave my apartment, march ten blocks uptown, and donate the bag of clothes to the nearest Salvation Army.

When I return home, I open my laptop and find the folder with the photos I took of the two of us. I'm tempted, so temped to grab a pint of Ben & Jerry's, run my fingers over the pictures, then download Skype and call his number in Europe to ask why the fuck he didn't show.

But I can't be that girl. I start my first job tomorrow. I need to be a responsible grown-up. I can't be the clingy twenty-one-year-old who isn't able to deal with being ditched.

I'm Penelope Jones, and I can handle anything.

I bring the folder to the trash, then I call up his contact information. His email address. His stupid phone number in Spain. I slide his name to the garbage can, too. My finger hovers over the *empty trash* icon for several interminable seconds that somehow spool into a minute.

But as I remember the way I felt last night, all alone at Lincoln Center, it's wholly necessary to stab the icon.

Let him go.

A clean break.

For the next ten years, I do my best to keep him out of my mind.

Until I see him again.

CHAPTER ONE

Penny

Present day

Shortcake runs free up the steps. She wags her tail the second her white-gloved paws hit the top of the staircase in our building. My sweet little butterscotch Chihuahua-mix glances back from above me, her pink tongue lolling as she pants.

"Show off," I say to her.

Her white-tipped tail vibrates faster and I take that as my cue to bound up the rest of the stairs, my heart still beating hard from our morning run in Central Park. Last summer, when I brought Shortcake home from Little Friends, the animal rescue I run—she'd insisted upon being mine, slathering me in kisses from the second she'd arrived—I never would have imagined she'd also demand to be my running companion. But she's a fast and furious little widget, all seven pounds of her. We're training for a Four-and-Two-Legs-Race that's part of Picnic in the Park to raise money for a coalition of local animal rescues.

When I reach the fourth floor, Shortcake scurries ahead, rushing to the door of the small one-bedroom we share in the upper 90s. It's all ours, and it's near work, so I can't ask for anything more.

With her leash rolled up in one hand, I unlock the door and enter my home. It's my oasis in Manhattan. The walls are painted lavender and yellow, courtesy of a long weekend when my friend Delaney and I went full Martha Stewart and turned the place into a haven of pastels. I'm not normally a pastel girl, but the soothing shades work for me in here. They make me happy.

I like being happy. Crazy, I know.

I fill Shortcake's water dish, and she guzzles nearly all of it down before sprawling on her belly across the cool kitchen floor, arms stretched in front and legs behind, super-dog style.

"By all means, feel free to spend the day lounging," I say to my favorite girl.

She flops to her side.

"I'm totally not jealous of your lifestyle at all," I say as I strip off my exercise clothes then go to take a quick shower.

When I'm done, I grab my phone. I check my daily appointment list as I blow-dry my dark brown hair. Normally, I'm based at the shelter, working with the animals and my volunteers, or heading to the airports to meet the dogs coming in from other states so we can find them homes. Today, though, I need to dress up and put on my best public face. My assistant, Lacey, has set up meetings for me this week with restaurant owners about catering the upcoming picnic. We're in a bit of a bind—the original restaurant slated to cater it had to cancel at the last minute. In a city stuffed with places to feed your face, you might think finding a restaurant is an easy task. But with a date a mere two weeks away, the options narrow quite quickly. So far, my effort to nab an eatery has been a big bust. I've been calling all over town in the last few days, but have yet to come across a restaurant that's both free that day and the right fit.

My quest continues though, since Lacey tracked down four restaurants with openings the day of the picnic. As I twist my hair into a clip, I click on her email.

First up is Dominic Ravini, who runs an Italian joint best known for its "heavenly" spaghetti, Lacey tells me. Bless her. But I just don't think spaghetti is right for a picnic, unless we switch it up to a *Lady and the Tramp* theme.

I peer over at Shortcake. "I'd share a strand of spaghetti with you anytime," I say as I dust on some blush. She thumps her tail against the floor. I take that as a *yes, bring me home pasta for dinner please. With meatballs, of course.*

Next, Lacey writes that I have an appointment with a burrito shop. I give the email a quizzical stare. Though Lacey assures me it's classy, I'm not convinced burritos are the best choice, either. I need to find a restaurant that can strike the perfect balance of sophistication and informality to entice the guests to donate to the shelters but still fit the picnic in the park theme.

That's why I don't hold high hopes for the Indian restaurant she has lined up. Big fan of chana masala here, but I'm not sure it screams *serve me on a paper plate in the park*.

As I reach into my makeup bag, I scroll to the bottom of the email.

The last restaurant with an opening is called *Gabriel's*.

I startle as I read the name and, unexpectedly, my breath catches.

That name.

I freeze, one hand on the mascara wand, the other holding my phone. Even now, years after my valiant attempt to erase that man from my history, his name alone does something to me.

I've dated since him. I've had a few serious boyfriends. But there's still just something about that man. Maybe that's the curse of experiencing the best sex of your life at age twenty-one. At the time, I figured that sex with Gabriel was so great because I didn't know better. Now, I've learned that sleeping with him was mind-blowing because . . . sleeping with him was mind-blowing.

Those three nights in Spain were magical, passionate and beyond sensual. I've tried to implement Gabriel amnesia, but he still lingers in the corners of my mind. Letting go of the mascara tube, I take a breath and tell myself a name is just a name. It's a mere coincidence that this eatery on my list shares the same name.

Except . . . my Gabriel was a cook. A struggling line cook in a small bistro in Barcelona that summer, planning to move to Manhattan for a job here.

I drop my forehead into my hand as a fresh wave of foolishness crashes over me. What if he's been here all these years? What if he came to New York and simply didn't want to see me? What if we've been sharing the same island for the last decade? What if he was married when we were together? What if he went home to his wife, his girlfriend, his lover?

I forced myself to stop playing this *what if* game ten years ago when he didn't show for our rendezvous. I booted him from my brain and refused to linger on him, and especially on all the possible reasons why he left me alone.

Now, he's all I can think about. I need to know if this Gabriel is *my* Gabriel.

When I google the restaurant, I let out an audible groan.

I blink.

Blink again.

Try to still my shaking fingers.

He's here. He's in Manhattan. After a decade, I'm going to come face-to-face with the man who stole my heart and my body.

I set down my phone and scoop up my dog. "Can I send Lacey instead?"

She licks my cheek in reply.

"Is that a yes, Shortcake? As in, you think I should play hooky and spend the day with you and make Lacey do my dirty work?"

This time she administers a longer tongue-lashing.

"Most of the time I'm completely content with the fact that you don't talk," I tell her. "But today is not one of those days."

The mere possibility of seeing him again sets off a storm of warring emotions and confusion inside me. I don't know what to do about this meeting, what to say to him, how I should act. The one thing I'm certain of is that I *need* a two-way conversation, so I call my friend Delaney as I pace around my small living room.

"Hey there," she shouts over the background clatter of construction. "If you can't hear me it's because they're jackhammering one frigging block away from my spa, which is completely conducive to a restful day of relaxation. Not."

I laugh. "Let me guess. You're walking to work."

"You got it," she says, her normally pretty voice blaring so loudly I have to hold the phone several inches from my ear.

"Speaking of guessing, want to guess who I just found out is on my work schedule today?"

"Tom Hardy? Scott Eastwood? Chris Pine?"

"Henry Cavill," I say, since he's her favorite celebrity. "But seriously, I'm supposed to have a meeting with . . ." I stop, since I can still hardly believe what I'm about to say. Then I use the nickname we bestowed on Gabriel many moons ago over a bottle of cabernet. "My *international man of mystery.*"

She gasps, and it's loud enough for me to hear her over the racket. "Are you serious?"

I nod. "One hundred percent."

"Okay, hold on," she says, and then ten seconds later, the background noise is sliced away and it's blissfully quiet. "I stepped into the ATM lobby near work. My first massage is in ten minutes, so give me the details."

I dive in and tell her everything I know. "What do I do? Do I go? Do I send Lacey instead? Do I just . . . *not show?*"

But as I say the last two words, I know I won't do that. I've been on the receiving end of not showing, and I won't stand him up.

"Simple," she says, with authority. "You go."

My stomach drops. Pressing a hand to the wall for balance, I ask, "Are you sure you didn't mean to say I should spend the day working hard at the shelter so that Lacey can have more responsibility overseeing our charitable events?"

Delaney cracks up. "Yes, I'm completely sure I did not say that. Especially since, correct me if I'm wrong, but this is your job, not hers?"

I heave a sigh as I nod. Backing out isn't my style anyway. This is *my* event and *my* responsibility. It's not something I can push off on an assistant who's still learning the ropes. Besides, with one cancellation already, I need to make sure Picnic in the Park comes together. The buck stops with me.

"Yeah, you're right," I say, resigned. "So, um, what do I do? I have no clue how to waltz into his restaurant like he didn't totally devastate me when I stood waiting at Lincoln Center for a man who never showed."

"It's simple," Delaney says in a cool, confident tone.

"How is it simple?"

"Because you're not the same person. You're not that heartbroken twenty-one-year-old about to start a job she did her best to pretend she was going to love because she thought it would please her parents."

"True," I say, some of her confidence rubbing off on me.

I've changed since then. When I went to Spain after college graduation, I was *mostly* sure that I'd be a research analyst on Wall Street. But a small part of me had dreaded that job before it had even started, and that was why I left after only six months. Funny thing—I wasn't the only one to take off from Smith & Holloway. That was the year of exits from the bank, and it became a running joke. First the receptionist, then the human resources manager, then me. "And I love my job now," I say to Delaney, giving myself a pep talk, "and that's why I have to meet with him. Because who cares about him, anyway? The event is more important than his stupid decision to walk away from me."

"Exactly. And you're not the type of woman any sane man should walk away from. So you need to make him eat his heart out."

"I like how you think," I say, a dose of confidence surging through me.

"Leave your hair down, show off that sexy new tattoo, and wear something that makes you look stunning. You look amazing in blue."

I laugh. "He used to say that, too."

"Boom. Done. Get out that royal blue off-the-shoulder top. The sapphire-colored one. Wear it with jeans. Women usually think they need to show their bare legs to be sexy, but a great pair of skinny jeans and heels is hotter than a skirt. Then walk in with your chin held high, like you don't care that he broke your heart."

A grin spreads across my face. "Perfect. That's the opposite of how I dressed when I knew him." I was all about sundresses and cute little skirts when he met me. Young and innocent.

It's time to dress like the woman I am, not the girl I was.

I say good-bye and open my closet. I want to be so god-damn memorable that his jaw drops from the shock, that he falls to his knees and begs forgiveness for standing me up, that he tells me he hasn't gone a day without thinking of me.

Oh yes, I wish for Gabriel to regret with every fiber of his being that he left me alone on what should have been the most romantic reunion of two summer lovers ever.

I slip into my favorite jeans then adjust the shoulder on the top to show off the lily tattoo on my shoulder blade. As I slide my feet into a pair of black flats, I grab my favorite black heels and drop them into my bag. No need to kill myself in four-inch shoes until I arrive at my final meeting.

On the way to my first appointment, I use my phone to take an online crash course in Gabriel Mathias. Since I don't follow the restaurant scene, I had no idea he'd set up shop here. Turns out he's now something of a rising rock-star chef, who recently won a season of a popular reality TV cooking show, then a few months ago he rode that spot of fame to open his first Manhattan establishment. It's the flagship for a bigger business he now runs in cook-ware, cookbooks, and more.

Well, la-dee-dah. The once-struggling cook who excelled at paella has gone from rags to riches.

I grit my teeth when I see the first photo of him. He's still gorgeous. Actually, I should revise that. He's even more gorgeous.

The fucker.

But I'm not going to let his looks soften me. I'm not going to be swayed by his pretty face. I'm strong, and I'm tough, and I'm smart, too. Which means I need to be prepared.

I find a clip from his show on YouTube as I walk along Eighth Avenue. Popping in my headphones, I hit play and brace myself.

Do not let that sexy accent woo you. Do not stare at those kissable lips.

I do my best to listen objectively, as if he's a test subject in a lab. A host or producer off-camera asks him a question. "You lost tonight's appetizer battle. What do you think that does for your chances to win it all?"

"It makes it tougher for me to win," he says in that warm, sexy voice I adored. "But I'm ready for the challenge. I'll need to work harder on the main course match."

I scoff as I march down the sidewalk. What will these reality geniuses come up with next? Salad showdown? Dessert skirmish?

"How did you feel losing to Angelique when you've been making a name for yourself as a master of appetizers?"

Gabriel takes a breath, his chest rising and falling. Then the corner of his lips curves up. "I was frustrated with myself but not so angry that I'd have, say, thrown a phone."

A laugh comes from off-camera, and I can only imagine the producers huddled together to try to incite him to throw a phone over a fallen flan, or a run-of-the-mill risotto.

The screen flashes, and the video clip cuts to what looks to be the end of the episode with the host holding Gabriel's hand high in the air. I guess he won the match in the end, and his phone was safe from damage.

As I stop at the crosswalk, I return to my original search. My eyes widen when I dig deeper and find stories of his official win on the cooking show, and all the names the media bestowed on him.

The sexiest chef.

The hottest cook.

The heartbreaker in the kitchen.

Nearly every article comes with a photo of him. I click on the first few. Then another set. Then one more group of pics. My chest burns with annoyance. My muscles tighten with anger.

In every single picture of the chef du jour, he has a different woman on his arm.

That's my answer as to why he never showed. Gabriel is a ladies' man. A bad boy. The consummate playboy, out with a new beautiful babe every single night.

As I head in to my meeting with the Italian chef, I hope against hope this man can do something amazing with spaghetti at a picnic so I can call off the rest of my appointments.

He can't.

Then, it turns out the burrito man is now booked for another event.

At the Indian restaurant, the manager tells me it would be his first time catering an event, and he can only cook for fifty. We're expecting more than three hundred. I thank him with a smile, then sigh heavily as I leave and head to the Village to see the man who swept me off my feet once upon a time.

As the train chugs into the station, I change my shoes then tug on my top, showing a bit more shoulder than I usually do. He *loved* to kiss me there. He loved tattoos, too. I didn't have any then. I have three now, including the lily. Let him look. Let him stare.

I slick on lip gloss as I leave the subway, check my reflection in the shop window on the corner, and make my way to Gabriel's on Christopher Street. My heart beats double time.

When I reach the brick-front eatery on the corner of two cobbled streets, I'm more impressed than I want to be.

His restaurant is so cool and hip and sexy, with a dash of old-fashioned charm in the hanging wooden sign.

I narrow my eyes, and nearly breathe a plume of fire onto the entryway. He probably charms the female patrons with his witty words, his panty-melting grin, and his fucking amazing food.

Then takes them to his bed and runs his tongue . . .

Stop. Just stop.

I clench my fists then take a breath, letting it spread through my body. I remind myself I'm here for business. I'm here for the dogs. This is my chance to raise a lot of money for a cause that matters dearly to me.

When the hostess greets me and I tell her I have a meeting with Gabriel, a part of me hopes that he's grown a paunch, acquired a receding hairline, or perhaps lost a tooth in a barroom brawl.

But as he strides toward where I wait by the door, the saying *take my breath away* means something entirely new.

Oxygen flees my body.

The twenty-four-year-old guy who dazzled me when I gave him my virginity a decade ago has nothing on this man in front of me.

He's as beautiful as heartbreak. With cheekbones carved by the masters, eyes the color of topaz, and hair that's now shoulder-length, he's somehow impossibly sexier. My fingers itch to touch those dark strands. My skin sizzles as images of him moving over me flicker fast before my eyes.

I try to focus on the here and now, but the here and now makes my heart hammer with desire. Everything about him exudes confidence, charm, and sex appeal, even his casual clothes. He wears black jeans, lace-up boots, and a well-worn V-neck T-shirt that reveals his lean, toned, inked arms. He had several when I knew him—now his arms are nearly covered in artwork, and they're stunning. His ink is so incredibly seductive.

He holds out a hand and flashes me that grin that makes me want to grab the neck of his shirt, yank him close, and say *kiss me now like you did all those nights before.*

Instead, he takes my palm in his then presses his lips to the top of my hand, making my head spin. Then he speaks, his accent like an opiate. He's French and Brazilian, and I don't know which side dominates his voice. I don't care, either, because the mixture of the two is delicious. "I've been looking forward to seeing you, Penny."

Oh God. Oh shit. He's excited to see me.

My stupid heart dances.

I swallow, trying to tap in to the section of my brain that's capable of language. I part my lips, but my mouth imitates the Sahara. I dig down deep, somehow finding the power of speech, and manage a parched, "Hello."

So much for playing it cool.

"Shall we sit down?" he asks, his delicious voice as sensual as it was that summer.

Yes, and tell me you're sorry. Tell me you were trapped in a cave, that spies stole your phone, that you were offered the job of the century in Nepal and you couldn't bear to see me again because then you'd never have taken the gig. You had no choice, clearly. Seeing me would have made it impossible to resist me.

Because that would be him eating his goddamn heart out.

Instead, I'm greeted with another enchanting smile as he says, "It's so good to meet you. I want to hear all about your charity and to see if we can work together for your event. My business manager believes this could be a great partnership for us both." He gestures to a quiet booth in the far corner. The lunchtime rush hasn't begun. I sit, then he slides across from me.

As I begin to share information with him about Little Friends, a fresh, cold wave of understanding washes over me.

He doesn't recognize me, and I honestly don't look that different than I did ten years ago.

Which means . . . he doesn't remember me.

ALSO BY LAUREN BLAKELY

Check out my contemporary romance novels!

BIG ROCK, the hit New York Times
Bestselling standalone romantic comedy!

MISTER O, also a New York Times
Bestselling standalone romantic comedy!

WELL HUNG, a New York Times
Bestselling standalone romantic comedy!

The New York Times and USA Today
Bestselling Seductive Nights series including
Night After Night, After This Night,
and *One More Night*

And the two standalone
romance novels, *Nights With Him* and
Forbidden Nights, both New York Times
and USA Today Bestsellers!

Sweet Sinful Nights, Sinful Desire and
Sinful Longing, the first three books in the
New York Times Bestselling high-heat
romantic suspense series that spins off
from Seductive Nights!

Playing With Her Heart, a
USA Today bestseller, and a sexy Seductive Nights
spin-off standalone! (Davis and Jill's romance)

21 Stolen Kisses, the USA Today
Bestselling forbidden new adult romance!

Caught Up In Us, a New York Times and
USA Today Bestseller! (Kat and Bryan's romance!)

Pretending He's Mine, a Barnes & Noble and
iBooks Bestseller! (Reeve & Sutton's romance)

Trophy Husband, a New York Times and
USA Today Bestseller! (Chris & McKenna's romance)

Far Too Tempting, the USA Today Bestselling
standalone romance! (Matthew and Jane's romance)

Stars in Their Eyes, an iBooks bestseller!
(William and Jess' romance)

My USA Today bestselling
No Regrets series that includes
The Thrill of It (Meet Harley and Trey)
and its sequel
Every Second With You

My New York Times and USA Today
Bestselling Fighting Fire series that includes
Burn For Me (Smith and Jamie's romance!)
Melt for Him (Megan and Becker's romance!)
and *Consumed by You* (Travis and Cara's romance!)

Sapphire Affair series…
The Sapphire Affair
The Sapphire Heist

ACKNOWLEDGMENTS

Thank you so much to my amazing readers as always! Big love to my husband, my children, my family and my dogs. I am grateful for the guidance of Michelle Wolfson and KP Simmon, as well as the insight into the story from Jen McCoy, Kim Bias and Dena Marie. Lauren McKellar works editorial magic and Karen Lawson is a goddess of precision. Thank you to Kelley, Candi and Keyanna. Thank you to Helen for the stunning cover, and Lauren Perry for the photography. Thanks to that sexy man on the cover for having a beautiful body! And thanks to my friends who keep me sane, though that's up for debate admittedly, every day.

CONTACT

I love hearing from readers! You can find me on Twitter at LaurenBlakely3, or Facebook at LaurenBlakelyBooks, or online at LaurenBlakely.com. You can also email me at laurenblakelybooks@gmail.com

CPSIA information can be obtained at www.ICGtesting.com
Printed in the USA
LVOW10s0355191016

509283LV00017B/500/P